EDITED BY LEITH MORTON

# SEVEN STORIES OF MODERN JAPAN

D0912343

UNIVERSITY OF SYDNEY EAST ASIAN SERIES NUMBER 5

EDITED BY LEITH MORTON

# SEVEN
# STORIES
# OF
# MODERN
# JAPAN

UNIVERSITY OF SYDNEY EAST ASIAN SERIES NUMBER 5

wild peony

Published by WILD PEONY PTY LTD
PO Box 636 Broadway NSW 2007 Australia
Fax (02) 763 1320

International Distribution:
University of Hawaii Press, 2840 Kolowalu Street, Honolulu,
Hawaii 96822
Fax (808) 988 6052

National Library of Australia
Cataloguing-in-Publication entry
Seven stories of modern Japan.

  ISBN 0 9590735 9 0

  1. Short stories, Japanese. I. Morton, Leith. II. University of
  Sydney. III. Title: 7 stories of modern Japan. (Series:
  University of Sydney East Asian series; no. 5).
895.630108044

*Cover design by Paul Soady*
*Set in 10/11 Times Roman*
*Printed and bound in Australia by NCP, Canberra*

# Contents

# Acknowledgements

We acknowledge the assistance of
The Japan Foundation
and
The University of Sydney
in the publication of this volume.

# Editions

*Three Policemen (Sannin no Keikan) Gendai Tanpen Meisaku Sen 10* ed. by Nippon Bungeika Kyōkai (Kōdansha Bunko, Tokyo, 1980), pp. 94-100.

*Sumida River (Sumidagawa), ibid.,* pp. 300-10.

*Road Through the Snow (Yukimichi), ibid.,* pp. 311-26.

*Happiness (Kōfuku) Nakajima Atsushi Zenshū* (Chikuma Shobō, Tokyo, 1949, 2nd edn.), Vol. 1, pp. 257-67.

*The Mummy (Miira), ibid.,* pp. 247-55.

*The Death of Osue (Osue no Shi) Arishima Takeo Zenshū* (Chikuma Shobō, Tokyo, 1979-86), Vol. 2, pp. 251-78.

*The Distant Garden (Tōi Sono u) Tsuji Kunio Sakuhin Zenrokkan* (Kawade Shobō, Tokyo, 1972), Vol. 1, pp. 295-302.

Japanese names appear in the Japanese order, with the surname first. Romanization follows the system used in Kenkyūsha's *New Japanese-English Dictionary* (4th edn, Tokyo, 1974), except for common place-names where the macron used to indicate the long vowel is omitted.

# Introduction

The stories collected in this volume span a period of over fifty years from the publication of Arishima Takeo's "The Death of Osue" in 1914 to the publication of Minakami Tsutomu's "Road Through the Snow" in 1976. The diversity of subject matter reflects not only the diversity in approach taken by their very different authors but also the remarkable changes that have occurred in Japan itself over the past half-century. Nevertheless the stories (here translated into English for the first time) share characteristics common to much Japanese fiction written during the modern era.

One of the most noticeable of these characteristics is the ubiquity of the first-person narrator. In the most recent three stories all published in the 1970s — Yoshiyuki Junnosuke's "Three Policemen" (1974), Shimamura Toshimasa's "Sumida River" (1976) and Minakami Tsutomu's "Road Through the Snow" (1976) — the first person narrator plays a crucial role. The particular approach to fiction signalled by the similarity in technique enables all three works to be categorized as examples of *shi-shōsetsu* (I-novels), the major tradition in twentieth-century Japanese writing.[1]

Noriko Mizuta Lippit discerns two distinct types of I-novel. First, there is the essay-like novel in which the author meditates upon himself with a "profound, if egocentric, inward turning eye".[2] The second type of I-novel Lippit characterizes as "confessional" and

---

[1] A newly-published study devoted to the I-novel is Edward Fowler, *The Rhetoric of Confession* (University of California Press, 1988).

[2] Noriko M. Lippit, *Reality and Fiction in Modern Japanese Literature* (M. D. Sharpe, New York, 1980), p. 14.

demonstrates how the perspective of such a work can be ironic, "creating a critical distance between the author and the protagonist" with the result that "the protagonist emerges as an ironic dramatization of the author, not as a faithful portrayal or subjective self-dramatization".[3] The significance of this genre of writing for postwar literature is even more clearly underlined by the use of phrases like *katei no jijōshōsetsu* or "domestic exigency novels" (defined as a sub-genre of more or less autobiographical literature) to describe novelists like Shimao Toshio (1917-1986) who have achieved great fame only over the past decade or so.[4]

An essay-like recollection about World War II, indisputably told from the perspective of an inward turning eye, Shimamura's "Sumida River" falls squarely into Lippit's first category. On the other hand, Minakami's "Road Through the Snow" appears to straddle both categories of I-novel since it is ironic and meditative at the same time. Yoshiyuki's "Three Policemen" differs most from a conventional I-novel. But it does not require much imagination to find common links with the other two stories. Quite apart from the pivotal role of the narrator, the impact of World War II on Japan surfaces once again as a major theme.

It can be argued that, since all three stories were published within the same decade and by writers of equally advancing years, an affinity in subject matter is inevitable, irrespective of any common connection in genre. This argument is reinforced by an examination of the driving force behind the I-novel tradition — the pursuit of the self.[5] This is a modern obsession that Japanese writers share with

---

[3] Lippit, *op. cit.*, p. 22.

[4] Kathryn Sparling (tr.), *"The Sting of Death" and Other Stories by Shimao Toshio* (Ann Arbor: Centre for Japanese Studies, University of Michigan, 1985), p. 1.

[5] Compare the I-novel's "narcissistic obsession with the self". Lippit, *op. cit.*, p. 36.

their Western counterparts. A comparison of these stories with three Australian collections of short fiction also published in the 1970s confirms this. Frank Moorhouse's *The Americans, Baby* (1972), Peter Carey's *The Fat Man in History* (1974) and Anna Couani's *Italy* (1977) are, as far as such a thing is possible, representative of much of the best of Australian writing during that period, and indeed are well on their way to becoming "classics". All three collections are concerned primarily with the identity of the narrator, the "discontinuous self". Moorhouse, Carey and Couani are, each in their own way, as equally obsessed by the notion of the "protagonist as an ironic dramatization of the author" as any modern Japanese writer working in the I-novel genre.[6]

The comment that contemporary fiction ignores national and linguistic barriers is made so frequently nowadays that it has become merely another literary bromide. However the revival of interest in autobiographical modes of fiction recently experienced in the West does not simply parallel developments in Japan but may indicate a convergence with a mode of writing that has been firmly in the Japanese mainstream for many years.

The notion of continuity implied by the I-novel tradition is given substance in Arishima Takeo's "The Death of Osue" (1914). The pursuit of the self, specifically of sexual identity, verifies the link with the three stories written over half a century later. Arishima's narrator is not the discontinuous or ironic self of modern discourse but an older self who in the celebrated words of James Joyce "remains within or behind or beyond or above his handiwork, invisible, refined

---

[6] For comments on the work of Moorhouse and Carey see *The Oxford Companion to Australian Literature* (Oxford University Press, Melbourne, 1986); for comments on Couani, see my "A Future History of Poetry in the Eighties or a Defence of Recent Seventies Writing in the Form of Some Poets Mostly Associated with the Red Press", *Her/e* August/November 1982, pp. 227-30.

out of existence, indifferent, paring his fingernails".[7] In reality Arishima, like Joyce, managed to escape from the straightjacket of naturalism, so the voice ever present throughout "The Death of Osue" sometimes slips into Osue's own childish accent, and sometimes into her brother's stern tones. But the sense of self, of a girl discovering herself slowly and then tragically, persists as much as the war-weary narrator of Shimamura's "tale" or the elusive, guilt-ridden voice that recounts "Road Through the Snow".

Tsuji Kunio's "The Distant Garden" (1945) resembles "The Death of Osue" more than the three contemporary stories. Once more the theme of self-discovery or self-realization is predicated upon a tragedy. Moreover, "The Distant Garden" also recalls the early Joyce with a precocious, even precious style that mingles naturalism with a self-conscious romantic *angst*. But, like all the stories discussed above, it shares a common theme with a common mode of narration. The two, in fact, are simply different aspects of the same phenomenon, as is often the case in fiction with an autobiographical persona.

The remaining two stories are quite different. Here no trace of the I-novel approach can be found. Nakajima Atsushi is shown in two different moods. In "Happiness" (1942) he displays a gentle, ironic humour rare in modern Japanese writing. In "The Mummy" (1942) Nakajima turns his hand to a ghost story or at least a tale with a sting to it.

Thus, the stories collected here testify not only to the diversity of modern Japanese fiction but also to the complex interrelationships which persist in spite of the boundaries of time and genre. It is perhaps these interrelationships which help define the sense of

---

[7] Quoted from "A Portrait of the Artist as a Young Man" in J. I. M. Stewart, *Eight Modern Writers* (Oxford University Press, 1963), p. 431.

continuity (whether of genre or theme) that is often seen as typifying the evolution of Japanese fiction over the past half-century.

Leith Morton

# The Death of Osue

By Arishima Takeo
Translated by Leith Morton

## 1

Osue repeated the word "depression" over and over again. It was a term she had picked up unconsciously at the time.

"Because of the depression my brother's got problems too. On top of everything else he's had to arrange four funerals between April and September."

This was the way she spoke to her friends. It was an impudent manner of speech for a fourteen-year-old girl but someone listening to her could not help but smile at the sight of her flat, mask-like face with its tiny, turned-up nose.

As might be expected Osue was not clear about the meaning of "depression". But in the small neighbourhood in which she lived people would greet each other this way as soon as they met. So Osue grew to feel that it was the appropriate thing to say. It was actually at this time that a dark, forbidding shadow appeared on the face of her hard-working elder brother Tsurukichi. Sometimes it remained there even after supper. She had seen her mother, when working at the sink, put the offal from the flounder aside to give to Kuro but then apparently change her mind and put it in the pot to be cooked. At moments like those she felt a vague loneliness, she felt as if something was pressing down upon her in pursuit. But her misery was hardly strong enough for her to be able to link it with the depression.

In her family her father, long troubled by illness, stood in the

1

forefront of those who from April had died one after another. Paralyzed on one side, he had been bed-ridden for eighteen months. For a small barber shop it was a burden too heavy to bear. Every time a customer came her brother used to say almost out of politeness that they wished him a long life of course but at his age and in his condition there was nothing they could do; they simply could not care for him and for him to go on living in that state was actually a tragedy. Her father was exceedingly stubborn and arrogant and his influence had spread throughout the whole house. After falling ill his selfish manner had grown even worse. All day long he would find fault with everyone and so even Osue's younger brother Tetsu would mock him by repeating to his face what a nuisance he was, exactly the same words of abuse his mother would use. Upon hearing this the invalid would jump up and down on his bed, oblivious of his illness. Consequently his truculence spread through the whole household and the days passed in mutual antagonism. Nevertheless when he died it was as if the linchpin had been removed. Even that irritating, asthmatic hack that Osue had wanted to strangle, when it ceased, left her with a profound sense of loss. She felt like massaging his back once more. Her father's body was carried out from the front of the shop on the afternoon of that day when, in spite of the earth being covered in snow and difficult to travel over, the air was pleasantly warm, and kites were fixed here and there like windows in the marvellously clear sky.

The next one to die was her second brother, a young man of eighteen having neither spirit nor strength enough even to sulk. Osue could not distinguish between when he was there and when he was not. On those occasions when she crossed the doorstep expecting some rebuke after having spent her time in idle play, she knew as if she already saw them who was in the house and even how they were sitting but he alone was completely invisible to her. When he was

2

there neither was he a help, nor was he a hindrance. If someone made an unpleasant face he would take it personally, leave his seat and hide somewhere. In two weeks he had ballooned up so much as a result of his beriberi that his eyes were completely blocked. He died of a heart attack, catching everyone unawares. It struck Osue as rather funny that this pathetic-looking brother of hers should die so swollen up. From the very next day Osue strolled about as calm as could be chattering as usual about the depression. It was midway through a June in which, rare for Hokkaido, a long spell of damp and chilly rain continued to fall, reminding one of the showers of late spring.

## 2

August was already half over when the heat suddenly struck the north country. As one would expect the shop became considerably more active. In the early morning the dry echo of a plug being driven into the bath in the bathhouse next door shook the gentle dreams of those asleep. Dazzling posters from the Tokyo Sumō troupe announcing a week-long season opened the tiny eyes of the boys and girls of the surrounding neighbourhood wide in amazement, Osue's first of all. The posters of the Kikugorō Company arrived from the Sapporo Theatre. Moving-picture advertisements were plastered all over the front of the shop, crowding the wall. After his father's death Tsurukichi had directed his energies into trying to change the appearance of the shop. To Osue's great pride the front door had been repainted with a new coat of blue paint and a lantern with the name *Tsurudoko* inscribed in red letters on its glass surface had been hung in front of their sign. In addition they had been connected to the electricity supply and as a result the job of cleaning the lamps which she hated had vanished in a puff of smoke. In exchange she had gained from that year onwards the new job of washing and pressing the *kimono* but she was delighted with the swap and did not mind in the

3

least her new responsibility.

She would boast among her girlfriends, "We've got electricity put on at home. It's really bright. You don't need to do any cleaning."

It seemed that since her father had died Tsurukichi had suddenly become in Osue's eyes a great man. When she considered that it was he who had painted the shop and had the electricity connected she felt that she could depend upon him in everything. He worked his short, honest frame hard with his sleeves tied back by a sash of Italian-style cloth that her elder sister had made for him. Osue's sister was married to a carpenter who lived in the neighbourhood and was the mother of a sweet one-year-old baby. Rikizō, Osue's chubby eleven-year-old brother, resembled none of his brothers and sisters. Balancing himself adroitly on his high *geta*[1] he combed the customers' hair for dandruff and parted their hair. When summer came custom would gradually increase. The shop would be busy until late at night and the sounds of laughter and clacking chess pieces could be heard well into the evening. Tsurukichi did not look at all like a barber. He dealt with the customers in an unsophisticated way. This had the effect of pleasing them even more.

In this cheerful house her mother alone remained indoors, moping about miserably. Until her husband's death she toiled without respite, not uttering a word of complaint. If the invalid asked in a sullen voice for something she would, without a single word, expedite the errand promptly and efficiently but it did not appear that this brought him much gratification. On the other hand he gave every appearance of rejoicing in the care lavished on him by his son who died of beriberi. Perhaps because there lurked in his wife's heart a certain coldness he

---

[1] A pair of wooden sandals raised off the ground by two wooden supports under the sole. The two supports can vary in height. Attached to the top are V-shaped thongs gripped between the big toe and the other toes and passing over the foot.

seemed to warm to kind-hearted people, much as one warms to a hot-water bottle. Plump Rikizō was his favourite; Osue rated next in his affection. Towards the two older children he adopted a distant attitude.

Since her father's death her mother's manner had changed so much that even she could see it clearly. Until then a stout-hearted person who rarely revealed the other side of her character, her mother suddenly became moody and meddlesome. She turned into a grumbler. Her likes and dislikes gradually grew more extreme. Osue could not bear to look at the way she continually found fault with Tsurukichi. As she was not as fond of her mother as her mother was of her she would occasionally get the sulks and say something provocative. Her mother would explode into a terrible rage and chase Osue out the front of the shop brandishing a pair of fire-tongs. After escaping, Osue would go somewhere to play for the day then when she blithely returned home she would find Tsurukichi waiting for her outside. In the living-room her mother would be weeping in frustration. Her tears were no longer directed against Osue but against Tsurukichi who, she argued spitefully, was out looking for a wife instead of working hard at home. On the other hand sometimes when Osue came home her mother would assume an ingratiating pose, as if nothing had happened, and despite the fact that it was before supper, would call in Rikizō from the shop and, including lame Tetsu too, treat them all to some delicious crackers which she had hidden somewhere in the house.

Nevertheless the family was rather envied by their neighbours. Everyone would comment that since Tsurukichi was such a kind-hearted and hard-working person it was only a matter of time before he expanded the shop from the back-alley to the main street. For his part Tsurukichi laboured steadily on, paying no heed to praise or censure.

# 3

The thirty-first of August was the second celebration of the Emperor's birthday; because, Tsurukichi said, they had not celebrated the first — the court still being in mourning — he closed the shop for the day. They carried out a grand clean-up throughout the whole house, the like of which had not been seen for some considerable time. Even mother, whose prejudice usually emerged at the mere mention of Tsurukichi's activities, this day worked in earnest. Half in fun both Osue and Rikizō helped in the cool of the morning. When they were dusting the tops of the shelves, things they had never seen before or completely forgotten about, would unexpectedly come to light. They scoured all the nooks and crannies, becoming covered in dust.

"Osue look! A picture-book's turned up!"

"That's mine. I wondered where it had got to. Give it here."

"What? Give it to you!"

Rikizō played with it, dangling it mischievously before her. Osue suddenly pulled from the shelf three glass phials coated in a fluffy grime. One large phial contained clear water, in the other two phials, one large and one small, there was a white powder which looked like refined sugar. Osue at once opened the top of the large phial containing the white powder, grabbed a handful and made as if to swallow it. She declared: "Look Rikizō. I won't give any to someone mean like you!"

Then behind her Tsurukichi spoke abruptly in a sharp voice quite unlike him, "Osue! What are you doing? You idiot! Licking at that stuff... you didn't swallow any, did you?"

Startled by his anger Osue confessed that she had only pretended to lick it.

"See what happens if you taste even a smidgen from that little phial, you'll drop dead right before my eyes. That stuff's dangerous!"

At the word "dangerous" his voice broke. As if he had seen some invisible menace his stern gaze swept across the room. Osue was strangely disturbed. She quickly jumped down from her stool and took charge of the baby brought by her sister who had come to lend a hand, cradling it on her back.

In the afternoon Rikizō was told to take the utensils kept in the household shrine and clean them in the Toyohira River behind the house. Osue, who had grown tired of working in the steadily rising heat, followed behind. Naked children frolicked in the water which flowed swiftly, like an abandoned cobalt sash, over the broad expanse of the pebble-strewn sandbank. When Rikizō saw them his eyes glittered in anticipation and forcing the utensils onto her he waded into the water exchanging greetings with his friends. Osue too, rather than doing the washing, settled down in the shade of the river willow and gazing over the gleaming riverbank sang a lullaby to the baby on her back. But gradually she was lulled by her own song and both of them, resting awkwardly, drifted easily into sleep.

Startled into wakefulness Osue saw Rikizō, his whole body covered by glistening drops of water, standing before her. In his hands he held three or four unripened cucumbers.

"Do you want some?"

"They're poisonous!"

But after her work and her sound sleep her throat was parched with a burning thirst. Vaguely, preternaturally aware of the terrible disease of dysentery which had begun in the slum districts of Sapporo, Osue took a pale white cucumber from Rikizō's hand. The baby on her back awakening to the sight of the cucumber wailed greedily.

"You're a nuisance, aren't you. Here have one!" exclaimed Osue and thrust out a cucumber. Rikizō gobbled down one after another as if he were drinking them.

7

# 4

That evening, united for once, the family enjoyed a happy meal together. Her mother, that day unusually relaxed, conversed pleasantly with Osue's sister. Tsurukichi surveyed the well-ordered living room with an agreeable feeling, his glance fell upon the shelf-tops and when he saw the phial of medicine on the top he remembered what had happened in the morning. He laughed and said, "You never can tell whether kids will do something dangerous or frightening. Osue this morning, she almost drank mercuric chloride... you know what would have happened if she'd drunk any, she'd be dead by now...."

He gazed affectionately at her face. Osue was indescribably happy. She could not control the maturation in herself of a consciousness of male attraction, be it of her brother or anybody else. Was it something to be feared or welcomed? Whichever it was she could not offer any resistance to that power. The thought that it would suddenly strike her made the blood in her breast throb quickly, violently, and she felt her face burn as if it were about to explode. The expression on her face on an occasion such as that would radiate out into all the corners of the shop, like spring itself. If she were standing then, she would abruptly sit down and if Tetsu were present she would embrace him, annoyingly press her cheek to his, hug him tightly and tell him exciting stories. Or if she was sitting she would stand, as if she had just remembered something, and dutifully help her mother clean the living-room and the shop.

And on this occasion too, bathing in the warmth of her brother's affection, she stood up restlessly. Then taking the baby from her sister, she smothered its cheeks with kisses and left the shop. The northern summer night cooled so rapidly that it was as if water had been sprinkled over it. The evening moon rose suddenly on the other bank of the river scattering blue light everywhere. Without knowing why, Osue felt in the mood to sing as she went joyfully out to the riverbank. Moonflowers were growing here and there about the bank. Osue broke one off and gazing at its phosphorescent bud began to sing softly a travellers' song. She had a fine voice, better than suggested by her appearance.

"O how do they fare, my parents?"

When she had finished her song, one flower slowly opened its sleepy petals as if prodded awake by her voice. Fascinated, Osue took up the song once again. One after another flowers opened majestically almost as if to burst into song themselves in time with her singing.

"O whom do they frolic with, my brothers and sisters?"

A sudden chill seemed to pass through Osue's body and immediately afterwards she felt a sharp stab of pain in her stomach. She thought nothing of it at first but when it recurred two or three times she suddenly remembered the cucumber she had eaten that day. Consequently her dysentery and this morning's mercuric chloride became one confused jumble sending her mind into a whirl and the sense of calm which she had maintained until then was shattered into a thousand fragments. Rikizō, too, had surely felt stomach pains just then. Assailed by forebodings that he might upset everyone, by the fear that in desperation he might confess that he, Osue and the baby had all eaten cucumbers, she rushed fearfully home. But thankfully Rikizō looked quite untroubled and with occasional shouts of laughter was engaged in some sort of sitting *sumō* match with his brother. Breathing a sigh of relief, Osue entered the house.

However the pain in her stomach did not ease. Before long the baby sleeping on her sister's knee burst noisily into tears. Shocked, Osue watched the baby intently. Her sister thrust her breast forward but the baby would not suck. Fearing, she said, that the baby would not take to the breast in a strange place, her sister hurriedly returned home. Osue saw them to the door, and, all the time aware of the pain in her own belly, carefully listened to the cries of the baby fading into the cool moonlight.

Even after she lay on her side she could not sleep for the worry that at any moment dysentery might strike her. Tired from playing, Rikizō slept as if he were dead, but Osue was kept awake blinking in the darkness wondering when he would awaken and begin to complain of his stomach pains.

Yet when morning came she had fallen asleep some time during the night after all. The events of the previous day were completely forgotten.

In the afternoon news came unexpectedly from her sister's that the baby was suffering terribly from diarrhoea. Her mother who loved her grandchild dearly left immediately. But that evening her beloved baby departed this world. Osue's breast was all atremble. In terror she began to pay close attention to Rikizō's behaviour.

When night fell Rikizō, who had been silent since morning, furtively called his sister into the alley between the bathhouse and shop. Then he searched about in his bulging pocket, so full it made one wonder what was inside, and pulled out a piece of chalk. On the wooden planking he wrote over and over again "31st August 1913" and whispered, shaking, "I've had stomach pains since morning. I went to the toilet five or six times. Mum's not here. I don't know what'll happen if I tell Tsurukichi.... Osue, on your honour, don't tell a soul about what happened yesterday!"

Osue did not know what to do. When she thought that sometime tomorrow they both would be dead, a feeling of helplessness, of despair, impressed itself firmly upon her breast, and before Rikizō could begin to cry she burst loudly into tears. Even Tsurukichi could hear her.

In spite of everything, afterwards Osue felt not the slightest twinge of a stomach-ache. However Rikizō took ill quite suddenly and after enduring the torment of severe diarrhoea dwindled to mere skin and bone, dying without warning on the sixth of September.

For Osue it was as if she were dreaming. Her mother, preceded in death by her favourite grandchild and then her child, succumbed to an attack of hysteria and for a time fell into an intense delirium. The malevolent stare of her mother, like an evil spirit in a dream, sitting beside dead Rikizō, was etched sharply into the haze of Osue's mind.

"You fed them something bad. You killed both of them. But you, you alone, go on as if nothing had happened! You'll never get away with it!"

Whenever Osue remembered those eyes, she felt as if she could hear these words clearly in her ears. She often went into the alley, tracing with the tips of her fingers the chalk-marks Rikizō had made, and wept sadly.

## 5

The barber shop which, thanks to Tsurukichi's efforts, had begun to raise itself out of the mire, was easily dragged back into the depths of the depression which had become worse than ever before. The disappearance of Rikizō's round chubby face alone dealt the shop a mortal blow. Neither Osue's mother whose hysteria was cured but whose mouth had developed a permanent lean to the left, thus making her look as if she had a naturally malicious expression, nor skinny Tsurukichi whose skin was the colour of wax though his cheeks were rosy-red, nor tiny, lame and withered Tetsu presented an exterior that could bring prosperity and warmth to the house. Despite his ill-health Tsurukichi, on account of his youth, was able to pull himself together and redouble his efforts in the shop. But it was pitiful to look upon his exhausted frame, drained beyond the limits of his strength. Moreover, her sister grew particularly critical of Osue.

Osue was saddened most of all by Rikizō's absence but the force of her vitality which seemed to burst forth from within did not permit

11

her to dwell on the fates of others. In the time that it took for the traces of the chalk-marks on the alley fence to fade she had reverted to her former lively self. In the morning at the window facing east she could be seen from behind doing the washing while singing aloud. So the first thing to break the monotony of the house would be the red colouring of underwear and sash. When it was decided to hand over their dog, Kuro, to the tanner on the grounds that all he did was eat, Osue was unbending in her opposition. Clinging to Kuro's neck, she would not be separated from him. She claimed that she would increase their income by devoting herself body and soul to cleaning *kimono* and stitching dustrags.

She actually did work unstintingly. In her heart she was pursued by the need to somehow compensate for her concealment of the fact that she had eaten the cucumbers. She gave up attending the night-school on Sundays which had given her so much pleasure and she had Rikizō's high *geta* lowered a little so that she could wear them while helping Tsurukichi. As if he were her special favourite, she showered Tetsu with attention. No matter how late the hour, Tetsu would wait for Osue to come to bed. When she finished work Osue would take off her white work-clothes, hang them on a peg, unwind her sash and without further ado join Tetsu in bed. If Tsurukichi listened while cleaning up the shop he could hear Osue's soft voice telling fairy-tales. Under the pretence of sleep her mother listened too, sobbing.

Osue began to wear a coat over her unlined *kimono* thus enabling her (since her back could not be seen due to the coat) to wear instead of a muslin man's sash which hung loose at the back a short woman's sash which she could wrap around herself only once. From this exact time onwards loud voices proclaiming a depression began to be heard. The temperature, which had risen as if it were its duty to do so, soon dropped and despite the fact that throughout the whole length and breadth of Hokkaido not even one grain of rice seed could be obtained the price of rice fell ominously. Osue often gossiped about the depression and how four members of her family had died between April and September but what actually troubled her was a hardening in the attitudes of her mother and Tsurukichi as a result of the depression. It was not that her mother had never scolded Osue crossly before but sometimes mother and Tsurukichi would quarrel with a violence not hitherto seen. At times Osue rejoiced in Tsurukichi's harsh treatment of her mother. But on the other hand, the plight of her mother was so pathetic it was unbearable.

## 6

The twenty-fourth of October was the memorial day of Rikizō's death. Osue's sister who five days earlier had conducted the memorial rites for her baby's death came that day to the barber shop with sewing. She spoke with Tsurukichi. Osue was in the best of spirits having been fussed over by her mother since she woke that morning. Even towards her sister Osue acted in a particularly attentive way, asking for her often. She cleaned the wash-basin chattering to herself.

"Please try this — it's only a small quantity but please try it!"

Turning towards the voice Osue saw that the advertisements for Angel Pomade and a small sample jar had been delivered. She leapt up and snatched the small jar from her sister's hand.

"Angel Pomade! Tomorrow I'll come to your place to have my hair done. I'll use half on mine and you use half on yours."

"You've got a cheek!" said her sister, laughing.

When Osue was indulging in this childish game her mother who until then had been silently engaged in the living-room underwent a sudden change in mood and gave vent to a burst of violent anger.

Poking her face into the shop she remonstrated with Osue in a venomous tone, "Clean up that wash-basin quickly! On a fine day like today why don't you clean the *kimono*? What will happen if it

13

begins to snow?"

Her bloodshot eyes, seemingly swollen with tears, glittered eerily.

"Mother, if only for Rikizō's sake, please don't lose your temper today," her sister begged softly, attempting to calm her down.

"Rikizō, Rikizō... you say it as if he were yours but just who brought him up? His affairs are none of your business. Tsurukichi, too, working me to death because of this terrible depression. Look at Osue though! Day after day, she gets bigger and bigger and lazier and lazier...."

When she heard this torrent of abuse her sister grew strangely sullen and left to go home without a proper goodbye. Osue stole a peek at her nonplussed brother and, silent as ever, burst into a flurry of activity. Her mother remained standing in the doorway, muttering. A glum silence, as heavy as lead, filled the house, right up to the eaves.

After finishing at the wash-basin Osue went to the front of the shop and began to clean the *kimono*. The air had a chill to it but the late autumn sunlight fell from a clear sky across the sliding door at the entrance to the shop. The odour of paint hung faintly in the air. Osue appeared to be quite involved in her work and with a slight flush to her cheeks set about laying out onto boards the various patterned cloths. Her tiny fingers, their tips pinked, ran skilfully over the blackened board. Every time she bent over and then stood again her body described a graceful feminine arc. Tsurukichi, who was in the shop reading a newspaper, stared untiringly at her, his spirits buoyant.

As he had business at the co-operative he had an early lunch and when he left the shop she was steadily working away.

"Rest for a moment. Have something to eat."

Hearing his gentle voice Osue glanced up and smiled but almost immediately continued happily with her work. At the corner he looked back. She was standing there, watching him depart. As he hurried along the path Tsurukichi reflected on how appealing she looked.

Not heeding her mother's call to lunch Osue threw herself into her work. Just then three of her friends happened to stop by. They asked her to come with them to watch a caterpillar tractor trial at the recreation ground. "Caterpillar tractor"... the very words provoked an intense curiosity in her. Intending just to go and see she untied her *kimono* cords, tucked them into her sleeves and joined her three friends.

Before the stern gaze of officials from the Hokkaido Agency, Railways Board and Prefectural Office, the oddly-shaped tractor clattered noisily along, moving a specially constructed barrier. It was not in the least exciting, but to play with friends out in the open at last was a rare pleasure. She was thinking that she would still like to play some more when she noticed how cold it had become and looking up saw a layer of grey cloud spread across the sky. It was dusk.

Startled, she stood rooted to the spot. Her friends were astonished at how quickly the colour left her cheeks.

# 7

When she returned the brother on whom she most depended was still not home. Her mother was quivering like a flame.

"You lazy good-for-nothing! Where did you get to? Why didn't you die and not come back?"

She shoved Osue, screaming at her, "Rikizō ought to have lived but he's dead. You! It wouldn't matter if you died! You lord it over everyone. I want nothing to do with you. Get out!"

Not unexpectedly Osue flew into a rage.

"Does she think I'll die because she says to?" muttered Osue to herself. Inwardly fuming she wrapped into a cloth bundle the *kimono* her mother had taken from the washing boards and folded for her and left the shop at once. She became aware of her hunger then but did not have the courage to eat before leaving. She did, however, have the self-possession to take on her way out the small bottle of Angel Pomade beside the mirror and slip it into her sleeve.

"Well I'll go to sister's and tell her just what I think of mother. Die, she said, who wants to die?"

With these words ringing in her mind as she walked, she arrived at her sister's place.

Although her sister usually came out happily to greet her, today the neighbour's girl of about ten whom they were looking after came to the entrance to meet her with a sad face. Osue, a little discouraged, went to the back where her sister sat quietly sewing. Feeling awkward, Osue stood there hesitating.

"Do sit down."

With a piercing glance her sister fixed Osue in her gaze. Osue sat down and, to pacify her, took the bottle of Angel Pomade out to show her but her sister did not even spare it a look.

"You were scolded by mother, weren't you. She came here looking for you just a while ago."

Her sister, concealing her anger beneath her mild tone, began to try to persuade Osue to resign herself to the inevitable. At first Osue listened in protest but gradually she was drawn into what her sister was saying.

"Your brother's shop is failing, you can't get by with just his monthly income. My husband gives what little help he can but as soon as the snow starts falling his carpentry business will be over. So from then on he intends to work mornings as a painter's offsider but whether that'll go as he wants is doubtful. Now that Rikizō is dead, in the future you'll have to take on an apprentice. Mother, like as not, will fall ill now and again and the cost of medicine, when you add it up, is enormous.

"Tetsu, too, because of his disability will be of no help whatever when he leaves primary school. Even in the district around here you should know how many families have been evicted since October because they couldn't pay the rent. If you think it's got nothing to do with us you're very much mistaken. And on this day of all days, the memorial day of Rikizō's death — what are you thinking of, from early in the morning, having the time of your life, you alone. It still wouldn't have made up for it but at least if you'd stayed at home and helped mother clean the household altar and cook the devotional food she'd have been really happy but, no, you're so selfish. You're fourteen now, in two or three years it'll be time for you to get married. No-one will want a wife like you. I wonder if you'll always be a burden to your brother, talked about behind your back, all your life leading a dull, monotonous existence. If you carry on with your selfish ways you'll end up with no-one at all caring for you."

In this fashion her older sister interrogated and censured Osue. In the end she herself began to weep.

"They say those who are lazy live long lives, your mother hasn't got long to go, if Tsurukichi carries on working as hard as this you never know when he might fall ill. And since my only baby died I've got no reason to live either. You alone are left, utterly unconcerned by anything.... Oh yes, I've been meaning to ask you this sometime. You didn't give my baby something bad to eat at the Toyohira River, did you?"

"Why should I?"

Silent until then, her eyes downcast, Osue responded in a pleading tone and once again looked downward.

"Rikizō was with me... and I didn't have any diarrhoea."

After a while she added this equivocation as if to justify herself. Her sister, her eyes full of suspicion, looked scathingly at her.

17

Osue, still silent, suddenly felt a strong sense of grief deep within her. She was struck by an overwhelming sorrow. Her chest tightened and she felt completely drained. No matter how hard she tried to prevent it her breath came in gasps. As soon as she felt two or three teardrops, as hot as fire, trickle down her flushed cheeks the dam burst and she collapsed into a frenzy of uncontrollable weeping.

She wept for an hour. Rikizō's lovely impish face, the innocent face of the baby licking its lips changed, when she tried to see more clearly, into her father's face, her mother's face and the face of Tsurukichi whom she loved so strongly. When this happened she herself was astonished by the flood of tears and she wept even more. At this point her sister began to grow concerned and tried in a variety of ways to console her but it was all to no avail. Finally she let her do as she wished.

When Osue had cried as much as she could, she quietly looked up, her head felt considerably lighter and her heart was filled with a deep, sad calm. One definite resolve lay buried within her. Her head was completely free of all obligations. In her heart she nodded sadly to herself, "I'm going to die." She murmured gently, "I'm going home now," and left.

## 8

Tsurukichi was delayed due to business and returned home after the lamps had been lit. The electric light was burning brightly in the shop, the living-room managing with that alone. Osue and her mother sat apart from each other, separate in the darkness. Beside the cupboard Tetsu was snoring softly, bundled up in his shawl. Sensing immediately that they had been at it again Tsurukichi tried to break the silence with some innocuous remarks but his mother would not reply as she served up a tray of vegetables covered in a napkin. He noticed at a glance that Osue's tray had not been touched.

"Osue, why don't you eat?"

"I don't want to."

What a lovely, sweet voice thought Tsurukichi to himself.

Before taking up his chopsticks he rose and went to the household shrine. As he paid perfunctory obeisance before the small, unvarnished wooden memorial tablet he was overcome by a deep sadness. His gloom was all too pervasive and so he switched on the light. The room was filled with a sudden brightness. Tetsu appeared to blink but quietened down again. Tsurukichi's mood grew all the more gloomy.

Osue took his tray to the sink and began to wash it. Ignoring his admonition to leave it until tomorrow she continued silent and unheeding. On her way back she went to the shrine, changed the wick and made a small bow before the tablet. Slipping on her *geta* she prepared to go outside.

Tsurukichi felt a certain unease and called after her. Osue answered from outside, "There's something I forgot to do at sister's."

He was overcome by a sudden surge of anger, "Don't be stupid! You don't have to go out as late as this. After you get up tomorrow will be fine."

To these remarks he added, taking his mother's side, "Everything you do is for yourself."

Osue meekly returned.

After all three had retired for the night, the rebuke he had uttered earlier weighed heavily on Tsurukichi's mind. He could not help feeling that he had gone too far. Osue lay as silent as a stone, curled up with Tetsu, her back to Tsurukichi.

Outside, the first snow of the year appeared to be falling. The night deepened into a bottomless silence.

# 9

The next day dawned onto the expected snow. When Tsurukichi awoke Osue was cleaning the shop and his mother was tidying up the kitchen. Tetsu was tying his school things into a cloth bundle beside the brazier in the shop. Osue took pains to assist him.

"Tetsu!" she exclaimed.

"What?" he asked but Osue did not continue.

"What's the matter?" Tetsu pressed her but she remained silent. Tsurukichi went to pick up a toothpick and noticed on the shelf in front of the mirror a small saucer which ought not have been there.

Around seven o'clock Osue said she was going to her sister's place and left the shop. Tsurukichi was giving a customer a shave at the time and did not look back.

When the customer had gone he saw at once that the saucer had disappeared.

"Mother, the saucer that was here... did you put it away?"

"What? A saucer?"

His mother looked in from the back of the shop, replying that she knew nothing about it. Wondering why Osue could have taken an object like that Tsurukichi looked around and saw it on top of a water-urn beside the toilet. Inside the saucer there was a little water with a white powdery substance stuck to the side. He thought no more about it and handed it to his mother to wash.

As Osue had not returned by nine his mother began to grumble again. He himself felt that when she returned he would have to give her a talking-to until she finally realized how serious things were but then the girl who helped at his sister's place opened the door and came in quite flustered.

"Uncle just now, just now..." she gasped out between breaths.

Tsurukichi finding this amusing, smiled at her and said, "What's the matter with you? You're in such a state.... You're not going to tell me your aunt died."

"Yes, Osue's dying, come straight away!"

When he heard this he was seized by an unnatural desire to laugh aloud.

"What?" he cried and asked once more.

"Osue's dying!"

Finally he began to laugh in earnest. Then he sent her home almost as if he did not care.

Caught in the throes of laughter, Tsurukichi told his mother at the back in a loud voice what had happened. Hearing the news her face underwent a total change of expression and she rushed barefoot into the shop.

"What! Osue is dying?..."

A sudden queer burst of laughter exploded from her lips. Almost immediately she grew sober once more. Then she burst into forced laughter once again.

"Last night Osue hugged Tetsu, crying, not touching her food.... Ha ha ha how could this happen ha ha ha ha...."

Hearing his mother's laughter Tsurukichi was gripped by a deathly shudder but he too was caught up in it and matching her voice said, laughing, "Ha ha ha what on earth was that girl talking about?"

His mother did not attempt to go into the living-room but stood there stupefied. Her eldest daughter rushed in barefoot. At that very instant, almost as if he had been slapped across the cheek, Tsurukichi was struck by the thought of the saucer he had seen just a short while ago. With a total lack of logic he concluded, "It's my fault," grasped his tobacco pouch and tucked it in his belt.

## 10

Osue had already been to her sister's once early that morning. She had asked if any medicinal cachets had remained from the time of the baby's illness, saying that her mother found powder difficult to swallow. Her sister handed her the cachets without thinking any more about it. At about seven Osue came with her sewing again and in the small room beside the front door spread it out. Various bits and pieces were stored in the cupboard there and so her sister often had occasion to come into the room but she noticed nothing unusual about Osue. It did seem as if Osue was concealing something in her coat but her sister presuming as usual that it was just some snack or other did not bother to ask her about it.

Approximately half an hour later it sounded as if Osue had gone to the kitchen to have a drink of water. Since her baby's death her sister had treated unboiled water as poison. She called out a warning to her through the sliding door not to drink any. Osue stopped at once and went to her sister's room. Her sister had been busy reading Buddhist sutras and when Osue entered was polishing the brass pieces. Osue helped her. For some thirty minutes while her sister chanted sutras she sat behind listening piously but then stood abruptly and returned to the small room. After a while her sister suddenly heard vomiting noises from the next room. She quickly opened the sliding door to find Osue prostrate with pain. Ignoring her sister's questions Osue suffered in silence. Finally, after her sister grew so angry that she struck her a couple of painful blows on the back, for the first time Osue admitted that she had drunk the poison which had been on the shelf at home. She begged her sister's forgiveness for the trouble she was causing her, choosing her home to die in.

Her sister rushed to the shop and in a broken, ragged voice told Tsurukichi everything. When he arrived at his sister's Tsurukichi found Osue lying on a bed in the small room, gazing at him with an unexpectedly peaceful expression in her eyes. He could not bear to look at her face.

Tsurukichi ran immediately to a nearby clinic looking for a doctor.

The staff in the dispensary and reception areas had just awakened. He begged them over and over again to come at once and then returned to wait. But after forty minutes there was still no sign of the doctor. Osue had stopped vomiting but her violent spasms began again. Seeing her lying on the pillow taking deep breaths, Tsurukichi could not contain himself. He set out once again, fearing the forty minutes wait might prove fatal.

Only after five or six blocks did he realize that he was wearing high *geta*. Cursing himself for his stupidity he ran the same distance again barefoot through the snow. Suddenly he became aware of a rickshaw beside him. Thinking that he had made another idiotic mistake he retraced his steps for two or three blocks back to the rickshaw depot. A rickshaw was available but the "boy" was an old man who looked to be much slower than Tsurukichi. The clinic was only a block from where he had turned back. The doctor told him that all the preparations had been made as they were waiting for him to bring her at once.

Ignoring the rickshaw Tsurukichi hurried back to his sister's place to find that things had calmed down. He felt unconsciously that the worst was over. Osue had undoubtedly confused the small and large phials and drunk from the large one. That phial contained powdered caustic potash. Surely that was the one, he felt, but did not have the courage to ask.

It took some time before the rickshaw for which they had been waiting arrived. At last Tsurukichi was seated in the rickshaw with Osue cradled on his knees. Held in her brother's embrace, she smiled faintly. His affection for his baby sister pulled at his heart, as if it were cutting into him. All he could think of was how he could give her life.

Osue was finally carried into a large first-floor room of the clinic and laid upon snow-white sheets. She was almost panting in her desire for water.

"All right, all right. I'll give you something to drink now."

Full of tenderness, the doctor spoke these words softly to Osue. His eyes never left her as he put on his laboratory coat. She nodded meekly. Presently he placed his hands against her forehead and stared fixedly at her. But then he looked back at Tsurukichi, asking, "How much of the mercuric chloride did she swallow?"

Tsurukichi thought to himself that this was the crucial moment. He timidly drew near her and placing his mouth beside her ear asked, "Osue was it the big phial or the little phial that you drank from?" indicating with his hands the respective sizes.

Her feverish eyes fixed on Tsurukichi, she answered, pronouncing the words clearly, "It was the little phial."

He felt as if he had been struck by lightning.

"How, how much did you drink?"

He asked the question knowing full well that it was futile, having already been told that even an adult who had taken two tenths of a gram had no hope at all. Not saying a word, Osue made a round circle with her index finger and thumb about the size of a five *sen* coin.

Observing this, the doctor inclined his head doubtfully and said, "A little too late, I think."

He had the medicine he had prepared brought to hand. A pungent odour, like that of a powerful drug, filled the room. As a result of this Tsurukichi's head cleared to such an extent that he wondered if everything that had happened until then had been a dream.

"It'll be difficult to swallow but force yourself to drink it."

Osue, without the slightest sign of resistance, closed her eyes and swallowed it in one gulp. Then for a time she fell into a heavy, laboured slumber. Gripping Osue's hand the nursing aid monitored her pulse. In a low voice she conversed with the doctor.

Hardly fifteen minutes had elapsed when Osue flung open her eyes

24

as if she had received a terrible shock. Looking wildly about as if searching for help, she lifted her head from the pillow and began to retch violently. Her stomach, which had received nothing since the afternoon of the day before, brought up only froth and mucus.

"Tsurukichi my chest hurts so much!"

Tsurukichi could only nod emphatically while he silently massaged her back.

"I've got to go to the toilet," she declared, trying to rise. When everyone supported her she sat up with a surprising show of strength. She would not listen to talk of a chamber pot and made her brother support her by the shoulders. When she announced she would go down the stairs by herself Tsurukichi carried her regardless.

"If you go down the stairs on your own, you'll fall and kill yourself!" he protested but Osue replied with the faint shadow of a smile, "I don't care."

Her attack of diarrhoea was extremely violent. With such a severe attack of vomiting and diarrhoea she had at least some hope. Her back convulsing in great waves of agony, Osue was panting feverishly, her lips dry and cracked, and her cheeks flushed with a lovely pink glow.

## 11

Osue stopped complaining of the pain in her chest, instead she began even more strongly to complain of the pain in her stomach. Her agony was pitiful. Ever courageous she said she wanted to use the toilet once more but the truth was that she had no more strength. She was lying on the mat; massive quantities of blood gushed forth from her bowels. Blood spurted copiously from her nose as well. Midway through her cruel ordeal — clutching at the air, tearing at the sheets — she fell into the chilling, terrifying silence of a coma.

At this point her sister, who was busy trying to raise some money, arrived. She tightly braided Osue's black hair, tangled like flax, so it

25

would not tumble everywhere. Everyone wanted Osue to live. Meanwhile, second by second, she inched towards death.

Yet Osue did not appear in the least as if she were struggling to hold on to life. Her firm, pathetic resolve tore at their hearts all the more keenly.

Suddenly she woke from her coma and called out Tsurukichi's name. He had been weeping bitter tears in a corner of the room and nervously wiping his eyes approached her side.

"What about Tetsu?"

"Ah yes, Tetsu."

At that moment his voice broke, "Tetsu's at school. Will I send for him?"

Turning her face away from her brother, Osue said faintly, "If he's at school then don't bother" — those were her last words.

Nevertheless Tetsu was sent for. Osue's senses no longer worked and she was unable to recognize him. Finally her mother who had been compelled to stay behind and look after the house in the others' absence arrived in a near-frenzied state. She had brought Osue's favourite smart *kimono*. She was absolutely insistent that Osue be clothed in it. When the others stopped her she begged them to let her at least drape the *kimono* over Osue and then she lay down beside her. As Osue was totally comatose the doctor let her mother do as she wished.

"It's all right. Everything's all right. You did fine. You did fine. You did. Mummy's here. Don't cry. Everything's all right."

Repeating these words, her mother rubbed her back. In precisely this manner at approximately 3.30 p.m. did Osue end her short life of fourteen years.

On the afternoon of the next day Tsurukichi made the arrangements for the fifth funeral. The small coffin and the equally small accompanying party of mourners made a dirty stain on the newly-fallen snow. Tsurukichi and his sister stood in the doorway of the shop and saw the tiny procession off. They had an excellent view of lame Tetsu carrying the memorial tablet behind the coffin, wearing the high *geta* left to him by Rikizō and Osue, bobbing up and down as he walked.

Osue's sister silently caressed her rosary. Onto the hands, clasped together in prayer, of the surviving family members — Tsurukichi and his sister — snowflakes fell, one after another.

# Happiness

By Nakajima Atsushi
Translated by Sakuko Matsui

Long ago there lived on this island a man of the utmost wretchedness. Since the unnatural custom of counting one's age did not exist in these parts, it is not possible to say precisely how old he was, but this much at least was certain: he was not very young.

Because the hair on his head was not particularly frizzly, nor the tip of his nose *completely* flat, the ugly looks of this man had become the object of universal derision. What is more, his lips were thin, and in his complexion there was no splendid ebony-like lustre, and these things made his ugliness even more terrible. He was probably the poorest man on the island. "Udo-udo", things rather like our curved *magatama* stones, were the coinage and the treasure of the Palau district, but of course, this man possessed nothing of the sort.[1] Since he did not even have "udo-udo", he naturally had no wife, for one could only purchase a wife in the first place with "udo-udo". All by himself, he lived in a corner of the store-shed of the first elder of the island, working under him as his meanest servant. All the meanest tasks within the household were imposed upon this one man. On an island full of idlers, this man alone had no time to be idle.

In the morning he would rise even earlier than the morning birds chirping in the mango thickets and go fishing. There were times when a big octopus he had failed to spear with his *biskang* had fastened its suckers to his chest and belly so that his whole body

---

[1] *Magatama* were comma-shaped beads made of stone, used as jewellery in ancient Japan.

swelled up, or he had been chased by an enormous *tamakai* fish and had barely escaped with his life back into the canoe, or he had come near having his foot trapped by a giant clam about the size of a tub. In the afternoons, when everyone on the island drowsily took a nap in the shade of a tree or on a bamboo bed inside the house, this man alone would be as busy as a bee, cleaning the house, building a hut, gathering coconut honey, twisting palm ropes, thatching the roof or making furniture. His skin was always dripping with sweat, like a field-mouse after a rainstorm. Anything and everything except tending the taro fields — decreed since ancient times to be women's work — this man would drudge at by himself. At last, when the sun set in the western sea and the big bats flew about the tops of the massive breadfruit trees, he would be given scraps of *kukao* potatoes and the bony parts of fish, food more suitable for dogs and cats. After that he would lay his exhausted body down on the hard bamboo floor and sleep, or in Palau language "mo basu", that is to say, he would "become a stone".

His master, the first elder of this island, was one of the wealthiest men throughout the Palau district — from this island in the north down to Pelelieu Island in the far south. Half of the taro fields and two thirds of the palm forests on the island belonged to him. In the kitchen of his house, plates of the finest tortoise-shell were piled high to the ceiling. Since every day he sated himself on such delicacies as turtle fat, sucking-pigs roasted on hot pebbles, "mermaids' foetuses" and baby bats *en casserole*, he was as lined with fat and as pot-bellied as a pregnant sow. In his house was treasured the famous spear with a single thrust of which one of his ancestors was said to have killed the enemy leader when Kayangel Island was attacked in ancient times. The "udo-udo" in his coffers were as numerous as the eggs the hawk's-bill turtle spawns at one go on the beach. As for his Bakaru gem, the most precious of all the "udo-udo", it possessed such virtue that even the saw-sharks leaping and darting beyond the reef would scatter and retreat in terror at a mere glimpse of it. The massive curved-roof meeting house, decorated with bat patterns, which now towered towards the heavens in the very centre of the island, the great scarlet war-canoe with its snake's head, a source of personal pride to every islander — the building of all these things had been due solely to the power and wealth of this great leader. The number of his wives, though officially one, could in fact be said to be limitless within the sphere permitted by the taboos regarding intercourse with close relatives.

The wretched, ugly-looking bachelor who was a servant of this great man of power, was of such mean social degree that he was not allowed to walk upright when passing in front of even the second, third or fourth elder, let alone the first elder, his immediate master. He was obliged, without fail, to creep by on his hands and knees. If an elder's boat should come up when he was out on the sea in his canoe, the man of low degree would have to jump from his canoe into the water. Such rudeness as saluting them from within the boat was absolutely impermissible. Once, chancing upon a situation of this sort, he was about to jump self-effacingly into the water, when he saw a shark. The elder's attendant, seeing him hesitate, grew angry and threw a stick at him, wounding him in his left eye. Since he had no choice, he jumped into the water where the shark was swimming. If the shark had been three or four feet longer, there is no doubt that he would not have got away with just three of his toes being bitten off.

Koror Island, the centre of civilization, situated far from this island to the south, had already been infected by bad diseases said to have been introduced by the white-skinned people. There were two of these diseases. One was the disgraceful complaint which thwarts the performance of the sacred, Heaven-sent mystery, and in Koror it was called "man's disease" when a man suffered from it and "woman's disease" in the case of a woman. The other was an extremely subtle sickness, the symptoms of which were very difficult to recognize; the victim would develop a slight cough, his complexion would pale, he would grow physically tired, and he would waste away and die before you knew what had happened. Some victims would spit blood, but some wouldn't. The wretched man who is the principal subject of this story was apparently suffering from this disease. He had an incessant dry cough and grew more and more tired. He drank mashed *amiaka* sprout juice and a decoction of pandanus root, but they had no effect at all. His master noticed this, and thought it very fitting that his wretched manservant should contract such a wretched disease. So, the servant got even more jobs to do.

The wretched servant, however, was a very wise man, so he did not regard his lot as particularly hard. He was thankful that his master, harsh as he was, did not yet forbid him to see, to hear or to breathe. He decided to be thankful for the fact that, no matter how many jobs were imposed on him, he was still exempted at least from tilling the taro fields, the sacred vocation of women. That he had jumped into the sea where there was a shark and lost three toes had the appearance of a misfortune, but he could still be grateful that the whole leg had not been bitten off. And even if he was suffering from the hacking cough of "the fatiguing disease", when he thought that there were some people who suffered at the same time from "man's disease", it meant that at least he had managed to escape from one disease. It was doubtlessly a fatal defect in his features that his hair was not frizzly like dry seaweed, but he knew someone whose scalp was completely hairless, like a desolate hill of brown clay. Certainly, it was a great shame that his nose was not flat like a frog trampled to death in a banana field, but there were two men with the "rotting disease" on a neighbouring island whose noses had dropped right off.

However, even for a man who understood as well as this the art of being contented, it was nevertheless better to have a slight illness than a severe one, more pleasant to take a nap in the shade of a tree than to be slave-driven in the open beneath the rays of the midday sun. Even this wretched man of wisdom upon occasion prayed to the gods: might the pain of his illness, or the hardship of his labour, either the one or the other, be just a little reduced. If this wish was not too excessively greedy, please....

The shrines at which he prayed and set offerings of taros were those of the Coconut Crab Katasus and the Earthworm Uras. Both of these gods were well known as powerful evil deities. Among the Palauan gods the good ones hardly ever received offerings, for people knew that even if they were neglected they would not bring down curses. On the other hand, the evil deities were always reverently worshipped and had offerings of food presented in plenty, because tidal waves, wild winds and epidemics were all attributed to their anger. Now, whether the powerful Coconut Crab and Earthworm deities had accepted the poor man's prayers or not, one night shortly after this he had a strange dream.

In his dream the wretched servant had somehow or other become the elder. He was sitting in the centre of the main house, in the seat where the head of the family should be. Everybody was readily obeying his orders. It seemed as if they were shaking with anxiety lest they should incur his displeasure. He had a wife. There were many maid-servants, too, busily engaged in preparing his meal. The table laid in front of him was piled high with pigs roasted whole, mangrove crabs boiled deep red and eggs of large sea turtles. He was surprised at this unexpected state of affairs. Even whilst dreaming he wondered if he was not dreaming. He could not help feeling a little uneasy.

Next morning when he awoke, he found himself lying as usual in a corner of the same old shed with its broken roof and crooked pillars. But, unusually for him, he had overslept, failing to notice the chirping of the morning birds, and he was given a painful beating by one of his master's people.

The next night he once more became the elder in his dream. This time he was not so surprised as on the previous night. His words of command to the servants, too, were far more imperiously spoken than the night before. As before, all sorts of tasty dishes were heaped on the table. His wife was a powerfully-built woman of beauty; and the new mat woven from pandanus leaves was pleasantly cool to sit upon and truly excellent. In the morning, however, he woke up in the same dirty shed as before. And all day long, as always, he was made to sweat and toil, and for food, he was given only scraps of *kukao* potatoes and the bony parts of fish.

On the next night, and the night after that and for every following night, the wretched servant turned in his dreams into the elder. He became more and more at home in his part. No longer as at first, did he make a shameful exhibition of voracity at the sight of the splendid food. He had frequent quarrels with his wife. It was already ages since he had discovered he could make advances to women other than his wife. Ordering the islanders about at will, he had them build boathouses and he performed religious ceremonies. At the sublimity of his appearance as he proceeded to the altar led by a *korong* or priest, all the islanders alike were lost in admiration and wondered if he were not the reincarnation of some ancient hero. Among the servants who attended him there was one who looked like the first elder, his master during the day. The man's apparent dread of him was almost ridiculous. Amused at this, he bade this first-elder-like servant do all the hardest jobs. He made him go fishing and collecting coconut honey. Once, on the pretext that the man's canoe was in the way of his vessel, he forced him to jump into the sea where there was a shark swimming about. The sight of this wretched servant's agitation, perplexity and terror gave him great satisfaction.

No longer did the exhausting toil nor the cruel treatment of the daytime cause him to heave a sigh of despair. No longer was it necessary for him to address to himself words of philosophic resignation. For when he thought of the pleasure of night, the hardship of day was nothing. Exhausted though he was after the hard day's work, he wore the smile of one of the world's happiest men as he hurried to this tottering, shabby sleeping hut to dream dreams of glory and luxury. In fact, possibly as a result of the rich diet he enjoyed in his dreams, he had of late become noticeably fat. His colour had improved wonderfully and the hacking cough too had somehow cured itself. He was a picture of health and regained youth.

Just about the time the poor, ugly, bachelor servant had started having these dreams, his master the wealthy great elder had likewise begun to have dreams of a peculiar nature. In his dreams, the reverend first elder became a wretched, poverty-stricken servant. Every conceivable task was imposed upon him — from fishing, coconut milk gathering, and palm rope twisting to breadfruit picking and canoe making. There were so many jobs, it seemed to him, that even a countless-handed centipede would have found it impossible to manage them all. The master who ordered him to do all these jobs was a fellow who, by day, should have been one of his lowest menials. And this man was terribly ill-natured and made an endless succession of unreasonable demands. He had been gripped by the suckers of a great octopus, his foot had been nipped by a giant clam, and his toes had been bitten off by a shark. As for his meals, they were nothing but potato scraps and fish bones. Every morning when he awoke on the luxurious mat in the centre of the main house, he was worn out by the all-night labour, and he felt a throbbing pain in every joint. As, night after night, the first elder had these dreams, his body came gradually to lose its oily smoothness and his distended belly grew slowly hollow more and more. Indeed, no-one could help getting thin on a diet of potato scraps and fish bones. While the moon waxed and waned three times, the elder grew pitifully weak, and he even began to suffer from a distressing dry cough.

Finally, the elder got angry and summoned the servant to his presence. He had made up his mind to punish most severely this odious man who so tortured him in his dreams.

The servant who appeared in front of him, however, was not the emaciated, coughing, timidly trembling, faint-hearted wretch he had formerly known. In no time, it seemed, he had grown plump: his face glowed and he looked to be brimming with vigour and good health. Moreover, his whole demeanour radiated self-confidence, and, though his words were respectful enough, one had to admit he seemed hardly a likely person to be content to be at another's beck and call. At the mere sight of his relaxed smile, the elder was completely overwhelmed by a sense of the other's superiority. Even the dread he experienced at night of the oppressor of his dreams came vividly back and filled him with terror. A doubt flitted through his mind — which was the *more* real, his dream world or his daytime world? It was unimaginable that an emaciated creature like himself, continually coughing, should rebuke so magnificent a man.

In words of such politeness that even the speaker himself was surprised, the elder turned to his servant and enquired how he had recovered his health. The servant told him in great detail all about his dreams: how he was satiated with dainty food every night, how he enjoyed a life of pleasant ease and idleness waited upon by handmaids and menservants, and how he tasted the Elysian joys with a whole host of women.

When the servant finished his story, the elder was very surprised. What lay behind the remarkable similarity of the servant's and his own dreams? And, was the effect of nutrition gained in the dream world upon the body in the waking world really so drastic? There was now no room for doubt that the dream world was as real as, or possibly more real than, the world of the day. Suppressing his sense of shame, he told the servant about his nightly dreams: how he was forced to do laborious tasks every night, and how he had to be contented with nothing but potato scraps and fish bones.

The servant was not surprised in the slightest to hear all this. With an "I-had-expected-that" sort of expression and as if he had been told something he had already known, he nodded magnanimously, with a satisfied smile on his face. Indeed, his face shone with a supreme happiness, like the happiness of a well-fed sea-eel asleep in the mudflats at low-tide. Perhaps he knew now, without doubt, that dreams were more real than the world of day. With a long, deep-fetched sigh, the wretched wealthy master looked enviously into the poor, wise servant's face.

This is an old tale of Oruwangal Island, a place which no longer exists. One day, about eighty years ago, Oruwangal Island, with all its inhabitants, suddenly sank to the bottom of the sea. Since that time, they say, there has been no man in all Palau who has dreamt such happy dreams.

# The Mummy

By Nakajima Atsushi
Translated by Sakuko Matsui

When the Persian King Cambyses, Son of Cyrus the Great and Cassendane, invaded Egypt, there was an officer called Pariscus in the troops under his command. His forefathers apparently came from the region of Bactria, far away to the east, and he himself had a particularly gloomy provincial air, having never grown accustomed to urban manners. There was something of the dreamer in him, and because of this he was always a butt for mockery in spite of his fairly high position.

About the time when the Persian Army had passed through Arabia and finally entered the land of Egypt, the strangeness in Pariscus' behaviour began to attract the attention of his colleagues and subordinates. Pariscus kept gazing at the unfamiliar scenery around him with a look of extreme bewilderment in his eyes, and would stand lost in thought, wearing an uneasy and worried expression. It was as if he was trying to recall something but just could not manage it, and he was obviously irritated. When Egyptian captives were brought into the camp, he happened to overhear some of them talking. With a strange look, he listened attentively for a while, and remarked to someone beside him that he felt as if he could understand the meaning of what they said. He could not himself speak the language, he said, but it seemed he could somehow understand their words. Pariscus sent one of his subordinates to ask if the captives were Egyptians (for the greater part of the Egyptian Army were mercenaries from Greece or elsewhere). He was told, in reply, that they were certainly Egyptians. He looked uneasy and fell into deep thought again. He had never before set foot in Egypt, nor had he been acquainted with an Egyptian. Even in the midst of fierce battles he was still absent-mindedly preoccupied with his thoughts.

When they made a triumphal entry into the ancient white-walled capital of Memphis, pursuing the defeated Egyptian Army, Pariscus' gloomy excitement grew even more noticeable. He often looked like an epileptic on the verge of a fit. His colleagues, who had laughed at him before, now began to feel a little uneasy. Standing before the obelisk which rose outside the city of Memphis, he read out in a low voice the pictorial letters engraved on its surface. And he told his colleagues, still in the same low voice, the name and the achievements of the king who had erected the monument. His fellow officers were all puzzled and exchanged glances. Pariscus himself, too, had on his face a very puzzled expression. No-one (not even Pariscus himself) had ever heard that Pariscus was well versed in the history of Egypt or could read hieroglyphs.

It seems that it was about the time that Pariscus' master King Cambyses, too, began gradually to be afflicted by symptoms of a violent lunacy. He killed Psammenitus, the Egyptian King, by forcing him to drink bull's blood. Not satisfied with even this, he now intended to insult the body of the previous king, Amasis, who had died half a year earlier. For it was Amasis, rather than Psammenitus, whom Cambyses owed a grudge. Taking personal command of an army, he headed for the city of Sais, where lay King Amasis' mausoleum. On arriving at Sais, he gave orders to the whole army that the late king's tomb should be searched out, and his body exhumed and brought before himself.

It seemed the Egyptians had expected something like this to happen, for the whereabouts of Amasis' tomb had been cleverly obscured. The officers and men of the Persian Army had to go round opening and checking, one by one, the many graves in and outside the city of Sais.

Now it so happened that Pariscus, too, was in one of these tomb-searching parties. Whilst all the others were fully preoccupied in plundering the countless jewels, personal ornaments and household implements which had been placed in the tombs together with the mummies of the Egyptian nobles, Pariscus alone paid no attention to these things, but wandered about from grave to grave looking as melancholy as ever. At times a light like a pale glimmer of sun in an overcast sky shone tentatively somewhere in the darkness of his expression, but it soon faded and he reverted once more to his original restless gloom. It appeared as if some problem was hanging on his mind — something he felt he was about to solve, and yet could not.

One afternoon, several days after they had started the search, Pariscus was standing all by himself in a very old-looking underground vault. When he had lost his colleagues and subordinates, and in which direction from the city this tomb lay — these things were not clear to him at all. All he knew was that, somehow or other, on awaking from his usual reverie, he had suddenly found himself alone in the semi-darkness of an old tomb.

As his eyes grew accustomed to the darkness, there dimly appeared before him carved statues and a variety of utensils scattered in disorder about the floor, and embossed carvings and mural paintings all around the walls. The coffin was thrown on the ground, lidless, and by its side lay two or three heads of clay images. At a glance it was obvious that the tomb had already been plundered by some other Persian soldiers. A cold smell of old dust assailed his nostrils. From out of the inner darkness a large statue of a hawk-headed god was peering at him with a rigid expression. On a nearby mural was a gloomy procession of gods with the heads of jackals, crocodiles, herons and other grotesque beasts. A huge faceless, trunkless eye, sprouting slender arms and legs, was also in the procession.

Pariscus, moving his legs almost unconsciously, advanced further into the interior of the vault. After five or six steps he stumbled. At his feet lay a mummy. Again almost involuntarily, he raised the mummy in his arms and stood it against the base of a god-statue. It was an ordinary mummy, of the sort he had grown tired of seeing over the last few days. As he was about to walk past, leaving it where it was, he took a casual glance at its face. In that moment, a sensation — whether cold or hot he could hardly tell — ran down his spine. He could no longer avert his eyes from the face of the mummy. As if pulled by a magnet, he stood motionless and gazed at the face.

How long must he have remained standing there like that!

During that period, he felt as if a tremendous change had occurred within himself. All the elements making up his body, it seemed, were violently bubbling and boiling beneath his skin (just as in the experiments the chemists of later ages were to try in their test tubes), and when, after a while, the violent bubbling had calmed down, everything had completely changed from its former nature.

He felt perfectly at peace. He realized that what had been worrying him so terribly since entering Egypt — what he had felt he knew and had yet found absolutely impossible to remember, like a dream one strives to recall the morning after — was now completely clear. "Was that what it was, then?" Unthinkingly, he addressed himself aloud, "I was once this mummy. There's no doubt about it."

As Pariscus uttered these words, he had a feeling that the mummy curled one corner of its mouth almost imperceptibly. Where the light had come from would be difficult to say, but just the face of the mummy alone was outlined in a faint glow and could be plainly seen.

And now, in the space of a flash of lightning that pierced the darkness, memories of a long past life flooded back simultaneously — memories from a time when his soul once lodged in this mummy.

40

Direct rays of the sun, seeming to scorch the sandy soil, the stir of a gentle breeze in the shade of a tree, the smell of mud after a flood, white-robed figures passing to and fro along a busy main street, an aroma of perfumed oil after a bath, the touch of cold stone as he knelt in the dim recesses of a shrine — a throng of recollected sensations rose vividly in a single moment from the depths of oblivion and overwhelmed him.

Could he have been at that time a priest at the Shrine of Ptah? Perhaps. He was not sure, for what now rose fresh before his eyes was merely what he had once seen, touched or experienced, but he could recall nothing whatever of his own appearance.

Suddenly, the sad-seeming eyes of a bull he had offered before the god as a sacrifice floated back to his mind. They were like the eyes of someone, he thought — of someone he knew well. Yes, there could be no doubt, it was that woman. At once, there appeared before him a woman's eyes, a face lightly painted with malachite powder and a slim figure, and together with these there came back the memory of dearly-loved gestures and a nostalgic personal odour. Ah, how moving were these memories! But how lonely she looked, this woman, like a flamingo on a lake at dusk. Undoubtedly, this was the woman who had been his wife.

Strangely enough, he was utterly unable to recall any names — names of people, places or things. Shapes, colours, smells and movements, all without names, emerged and vanished in an instant amid an extraordinary stillness in which ideas of distance and time were strangely confounded.

He no longer saw the mummy. Perhaps his soul had slipped out of his body and entered the mummy.

Again, a scene appeared. He was lying in bed with a high fever, it seemed. By his side his wife's anxious face was watching him. Behind her there seemed to be more people — old men and children.

He was terribly thirsty. He waved his hand and his wife drew near at once and gave him a drink of water. After that he dozed off for a while. When he awoke, his fever had already completely subsided. He opened his eyes slightly and saw his wife weeping by his side. Behind her the old men, too, seemed to be weeping. All of a sudden, a massive dark shadow hung over him like a rain cloud swiftly darkening the surface of a lake. With a giddy sensation of falling, he instinctively closed his eyes.

Thereupon his recollections of that former existence abruptly ceased. And, after that, for how many hundreds of years did the darkness of his senses continue? At any rate, when he came to himself again (that is to say, in the present), he was standing as a Persian soldier (having already lived as a Persian for several decades) in front of the mummy of his former body.

Shaken though he was by this revelation of an uncanny mystery, his soul had now the crystal clarity and tensity of ice on a lake in the northern winter. It still continued to gaze fixedly into the depths of the buried memories of his former life. There, like those blind fish which emit a light of their own in the darkness of the deep sea, a number of the experiences of that former life lay soundlessly asleep.

And then, in the depths of the darkness, his soul's eye lighted upon an uncanny picture of himself in those days.

He stood there, in that previous life, face to face with a mummy in a dim, small room. Trembling with fear, the self of that former life had to admit that the mummy was his own body of a yet earlier existence. Amid the same dim darkness, faintly chill air and dusty odour as now, the self of the previous existence recalled suddenly the life he had lived in the life before....

He stood rooted to the ground in fright. This dreadful coincidence — whatever did it mean? If he continued to observe, calmly and closely, might he not find, amid the memories of this preceding former life

42

which he was evoking in his last former life, the same picture of himself again in a life which preceded the preceding former life? Might it not be that a ghastly series of memories, folding into each other without end like the reflected selves of two opposing mirrors, might continue infinitely — infinitely until the head reeled?

Pariscus, feeling his flesh creep, made to run away. But his legs were powerless. He was still unable to take his eyes away from the mummy's face. In a frozen posture, he stood face to face with the amber-coloured, withered corpse.

On the next day, when some Persian soldiers from another unit found Pariscus, he was prostrate on the ground in the underground chamber of the old tomb, and his arms were tightly embracing the mummy. With difficulty he was nursed back to life, but he now showed obvious signs of insanity and began to talk deliriously. And his words were not Persian, it is said. He spoke only Egyptian.

# The Distant Garden

By Tsuji Kunio
Translated by Leith Morton

It was a still, snowy evening; I was staring at the flame in the heater, my mind wandering, my eyes sore from reading. I could hear the faint sound of boiling water. It was almost eleven.

I had gone to the door a number of times intending to go to my bedroom but the shrill voice of my mother and the low voice of my father quarrelling in the living-room filled me with a wordless unease and I was unable to open the door.

In the room where the curtains hung heavily the glass window-pane coldly sucked the chill from the night and in its transparent crystalline depths illuminated the muddy glow cast by the street light. The light shone weakly on the snow, floating dimly out of the darkness, which covered the shrubbery. Staring, unmoving, I was seized by a terrible panic. I opened the door in an attempt to escape. A sudden draught of cold air from the hallway struck me in the face.

My slippers muffling any noise, I shuffled two or three paces in the direction of the stairs. It was then that I heard my mother sobbing. I stood absolutely still. In the shadowy light from the light bulb the door to the living-room was closed upon a grim, milky silence. The palm tree stood dark on the marble flagstones....

I ascended the stairs, all the while conscious of the silent movement of my shadow. All that was left was my constant isolation.

I remember. The icy atmosphere at that time, and in the middle of it, I built a tiny kingdom within me and cultivated it all alone. I loved flowers. They were the princesses of my kingdom. I played

44

with the light and chased the wind. They, the princes of my kingdom, comforted me in my loneliness.

My bedroom curtains were drawn solidly shut. Discovering myself standing there vacantly in that cave-like room, I felt completely alone.

When I climbed into bed, without any conscious volition, tears trickled down my cheeks.

In the morning too, it was snowing. I had a holiday from school. With neither my father nor my mother at home, it felt as silent as if the house were deserted. I sat on a chair in the living-room and listened to some old records on the gramophone. The austere pattern on the iron grating resembled that on the portals of hell, the flames flickered with a bright heat. I was downcast. I knew that last night my mother's bed had been empty. And that in the early hours of the morning my father was alone.

I did not know the reason for this. But sometime earlier a disagreeable tension had come into my love for my parents; I even felt some antipathy towards them.

Years later I was told what had happened. My mother had gone abroad with a musician. Even that, at the time, I believe I knew though my understanding was imperfect.

In the afternoon the snow eased and a wind sprang up. Otoshi brought afternoon tea to try to cheer me up. I was not pleased. I spoke harshly to this beautiful maid who had only just arrived.

It was about nine when my father returned, just when I was about to go to bed.

—Your father is calling.[1]

Announced Otoshi at my doorway.

---

[1] The use of dashes, the usual practice in France, to indicate dialogue reflects Tsuji's own deliberate stylistic choice.

—Haru-chan.[2]

I heard my father's voice from the back. I was overcome by anxiety. But my father smiled, standing on the earthen floor of the back entranceway.

—Were you asleep? How about it? What about making a snowman?

—A snowman?

Astonished, I peered at my father's face. As I stared at him intently his smile invited a warm smile back from me.

—I'll be there in a minute.

I replied and quickly changed my clothing, picked up my overcoat and stepped onto the snow at the back door. The reflection from the snow bathed everything in a blue light, things appeared clear and black in outline. The road had a slight incline but not enough to be called a slope. The branches of the chinquapin tree were suspended starkly against the night sky.

Puffing energetically, my father rolled up a snowball about a metre in diameter. I ran to his side. With joy welling up inside me, never having experienced such intimacy before, I asked, trying to draw closer to him.

—Does it have to be that big?

—Yes. Tonight the snow is deep so together we have to make a big one.

Spitting on my palms I made a small snowball and began to roll it near my feet.

Twenty centimetres, thirty centimetres, the snowball grew visibly in size, and as it rolled further, it grew larger still. My fingers felt frozen. Now and again I licked them with my warm tongue. My sticky saliva stuck like sugar in between my fingers. I wanted to call

---

[2] Chan is an affectionate diminutive often used when speaking with children.

my father. But I felt a certain awkwardness and, saying nothing, rolled my snowball along with renewed energy.

—That's enough. Okay. That's fine.

Father's words were given in a tone of command. The biggest snowball rose higher than my father's waist.

—Let's roll it to beneath the stone wall.

Together we rolled the two snowballs, one big and one small.

—Will it go on top?

—Certainly.

—Is it heavy?

—Uh huh. Right, up she goes.

I pushed with all my strength beneath my father's hands. The finished snowman stood as high as his shoulders.

—We did it!

A feeling of satisfaction as if I had completed something important would not let me remain calm.

—What about the face? Will we use charcoal?

—Let me think.

When my father had made the neck he straightened up.

—Hey, let's make a likeness of someone.

—Can you?

—No problem.

—Who then?

—How about you?

—No, not me.

—Why not?

—I don't know but no!

I kicked the base of the snowman with the tip of my shoe. And then I said as if it had just occurred to me:

—What about mother?

I was surprised at myself and uneasy. Overcome by a sudden urge to burst into tears.

—Fine.

My father responded to my suggestion with light-hearted acceptance.

—You do some work too.

On the verge of tears I buried my face in the snow, urged on by the pity I would feel for him if I did not. When I raised my head I had assumed a cheerful manner once more. He made the eyes and nose, putting the finishing touches to the whole figure. He seemed to me unusually enthusiastic. As I gazed, enraptured by it, the shape of the snowman took on, in some indefinable way, the appearance of my mother.

—It sure looks like her. You did a great job, dad.

I said and stood beside him for some time, scrutinizing the movement of his hands.

That evening I went to bed at a late hour. I slept with my father in the same bed.

The next morning the sky was a dazzling blue. The sun shone brightly, reflected by the snow. I rose early and went to see the snowman. It did not look as much like my mother as it had in the evening. Yet, even so, I could detect a certain likeness. I stood there for some time.

Then one month later, on a certain Saturday, when spring seemed at last to have arrived, I was returning home in the afternoon on the near-deserted Yamanote line. I had just passed through the ticket turnstiles at Higashi-Nakano station and was about to go down the steps.

I stopped in surprise. Standing there staring at me was my mother. An emotion almost of fear would not allow me to move. More surprising still was that my mother was wearing western-style clothing.

—Haru.

My mother was smiling. I descended the steps, powerlessly, as if pulled.

—What's the matter? Do you feel sick?

—No.

My gaze directed downwards, I said nothing.

Why was I afraid when I saw my mother? Why, as I approached my mother, was I gradually overcome by a deep sense of sorrow? I did not understand. Understanding was beyond me.

Still not uttering a word I began to cry. I buried my face in her overcoat and kept on crying, my grief unassuaged by my tears.

Even now the memory remains untouched in my mind. That emotion bordering on fear the instant I saw my mother. It was perhaps an involuntary reaction triggered by my being in my father's care. However even today it lives within me: the fear of something disrupting my kingdom, something over which I could exercise no control. As long as I hold onto this garden I have cultivated within myself, will I ever be able to direct my love towards another?

My face buried in my mother's side, still sobbing, I continued walking towards home. I crossed the overpass and walked along the narrow road lined by orange trees, my mother comforting me. I was tired out, as if I had cried myself to a state of exhaustion. Supported by her arm I smelled her sweet fragrance.

The figure of the snowman beneath the stone wall had long vanished. But a mound of mud-covered snow remained hard, like a rock, in the shade. Clinging closely to my mother, I said:

—Mother, I made a snowman with father just here.

—Really.

She turned and looked at the side of the road.

—Then father carved your face in it. It looked just like you.

She stared at me in silence for a time.

—Be a good boy, won't you?

When we came to the entrance mother spoke.

—I'm only going as far as this. We'll meet again. Take good care of yourself. Make sure that you do what your father tells you.

I nodded.

—We'll meet again. Goodbye.

She touched her cheek to mine and left. It was the time when the plum trees in the garden were soon to flower.

Ten years have passed. I have not seen my mother since. At times the need to see her is unbearable. I often weep on those occasions. But equally frequent are the times when I have not wanted to see her. The image of my mother ten years past whom I have hated but continued to love persists, like a marble statue, far beyond my love.

In the afternoons on gloomy, overcast days in the snow-covered north I often meditate upon my own gloom which so resembles this environment. It is surely only natural that I, unable to abide a constant love, should therefore not be able to love even myself. My final effort to believe in myself may well come to an end at some time in the future. Every snowy night I try to recall that garden in the heart of my childhood, all the while conscious of my fate in the face of my distant mother.

O sad light
The wind has blown, white, over the surface of the field
How far away it is... my childhood
The tears of that day
Linger in the wayside grasses
How sad, my mother
Whom I hated in my childhood

# Three  Policemen

By Yoshiyuki Junnosuke
Translated by Hugh Clarke

I started the best argument I have had for years in a bar with a man a good twenty years my junior.

Miki was with me at the time. An hour before we had been in another bar. The club was virtually filled with customers. Miki is small with a slight squint, but has long shoulder-length hair and a coquettish face which stand out in a crowd. We were sitting together with our backs to the wall. In front of us sat one of the girls from the bar. Miki gave me a wink, a signal that we should begin. I nodded. Then brushing up Miki's long hair I began, one by one, to undo the buttons running down the back of Miki's dress from neck to waist. I undid them all. Then still sitting alongside Miki, I touched the collar of the dress with my hand. The garment immediately slipped down over Miki's bare shoulders and fell forward. Unrestrained by any bra, the curves of Miki's breasts were revealed for all to see. They were quite large with beautiful pale pink nipples.

"Uh? Hey!"

The girl in front of us just gasped and sat there looking as flustered as if she had been laid bare herself. Soon the customers realized what had happened and for a moment a hush fell over the room. Miki took a deep breath and arched forward, giving a seductive smile.

The manager, in black evening dress, came rushing over.

"If you don't mind! This is no joking matter!"

"Why not?"

"What do you mean. 'Why not?' We can't have young ladies suddenly doing this sort of thing."

"Young ladies?"

So saying I stroked Miki's breasts, at which Miki wriggled and gave a squeal of delight.

"Come now. We can't stand for this!" said the manager.

"Can't stand for it, eh? Well, I suppose not."

I pulled up Miki's dress again and slowly did up the buttons. A rustle of talk ran through the bar and sighs could be heard from some of the customers.

"Nice breasts, don't you think?"

"Y... yes, but..."

The girl in front of us looked as if she was trying to fathom the meaning of our extraordinary behaviour.

I said, "I suppose you'd disapprove, would you, if a man with breasts like a woman exposed his chest like that?"

And Miki chimed in, "What a thing to say! Don't make things so complicated. I'm a woman all right!"

As soon as Miki spoke the game was up. It was a typical gay-boy voice.

"Uh?..."

Once again the girl looked surprised. Later, no doubt the truth would have spread through the bar.

Miki stood up and urged me on, "Let's go to another place."

Miki was something of a drinking mate of mine and it had become a kind of ritual for him to expose his breasts at every place we went to.

We were just about to go downstairs into a little basement bar, when Miki said with obvious dissatisfaction, "Oh, we goin' in here?"

The bar was tiny. Just the mama-san and a bar-tender. We were well known there, so Miki's little show would just be for the customers and there were precious few of them anyhow.

"You've had enough, haven't you? I'm tired tonight. Let's just have a quiet drink."

When I opened the door, there, right in front of me, was this young friend of mine. He was with two other fellows of the same age whom I knew vaguely by sight.

We got into a discussion with these young men. When your mind is fuddled with drink you can't think clearly. The point of the argument wanders all over the place and it takes you ages to make any headway at all. You suddenly realize that an hour has gone past, but the discussion is still revolving around more or less the same point. It's ridiculous.

It was ridiculous, too, how we got into an argument over whether or not you could bend a spoon with psychic powers.

When I said it was only a trick, the other three combined to attack me, saying that my views were a clear indication of senility.

It transpired that my young friend had recently got himself sandwiched in an entanglement between two girls. Apparently when he was in his cups he would sometimes break down and cry about it. I was surprised to hear that. Worry about women is a concomitant part of all men's lives. Lots of men are crying inside. But they don't let things rest there. They go out and try to deal with the problem. It vexed me to have this fellow, who was obviously still just a child, accuse me of being senile.

"There are human powers which haven't been developed yet."

"I'm not denying that. But that's not what happens with the spoon. You can't use willpower to make a clock turn backwards, can you?"

"But the spoon actually does bend, doesn't it?"

"That's because force is applied somewhere."

I demonstrated by bending two or three of the bar's spoons.

"That's what I mean by senility. Life is richer if you believe they bend through supernatural force."

"If you think life can be made richer by spoons bending, you're pretty pathetic!"

Beside me Miki yawned.

I tried to change the tack of the conversation.

"I'm glad we've only been talking about spoons. If we'd been talking about something else things might have been a lot worse. Do you want to go back to the war years and put us all in uniform?"

But the others weren't going to fall for that. Suddenly Miki said, "I adore uniforms."

"Why?"

"They turn me on."

"That's not what I mean. Would you like having to wear one yourself?"

"I'd hate that."

"But why do uniforms turn you on, anyway?"

"They look so impressive."

"What about police uniforms? Do they look impressive? And sailors' uniforms? They're pretty miserable."

"But they still turn me on."

I thought he must sense the group behind the uniform. The sweaty masculinity of a group composed entirely of men. Miki was drunk too. There would have been no point in explaining this idea to him. Anyway, no matter what we talked about, nothing fitted properly into place and the argument followed no logical course. Only the time flowed along unimpeded.

It was already almost 3.00 a.m. and everything had been cleared off the tables. The conversation was becoming increasingly fragmented. One of the three young men inadvertently came out with the hackneyed old line.

"The oldies were pretty slack during the war."

"You think so? You guys believe in spoons bending. If you'd been around during the war, I'm sure you'd've believed the *kamikaze* divine wind would blow you victory."

As soon as I'd made this reply it occurred to me that during the war I was only a boy myself.

"I was only a kid at the time, but I don't think you can necessarily say that."

I was not angry so my words were not as barbed as they might have been, but I felt irritated. When one of the boys said, "It was no big deal being in the war," my sense of irritation increased.

"Perhaps you're right. But life in wartime is lousy, I can tell you. Every night you have air raid sirens blaring away. Even if you don't go into the shelters every time, the sirens wake you up all right. And you might end up waiting an hour or more for a train."

As I was defending in this vein, the door burst open. There appeared before us a strapping young policeman. Actually, there were three policemen, but in the narrow doorway they were standing one behind the other. They just stood there in the doorway without coming in.

"What are you doing?"

The mama-san went trotting up to the door and said, "They're just leaving. Having a chat."

The policemen cast a glance over the tables.

"No alcohol, eh? It's late. You'd better be getting home."

Whereupon they simply vanished. All the three policemen cared about was whether the bar was trading out of hours.

"They sure let us off easily. They've got their own lives to lead too. They prefer not to have to investigate complaints either. But, if this had been wartime we'd have been in for it. We'd have been whisked off to the police station for holding an unauthorized meeting and plotting in a secret underground room. We might even have been tortured."

The three young men were not in the least moved at my words.

Miki, holding a cigarette burnt down low between his fingers, said, "Uniforms have oomph. They really turn me on."

He then sank back immobile into the depths of the sofa.

# Sumida River

By Shimamura Toshimasa
Translated by Hugh Clarke

## 1

The voice calling me gradually seems to be fading into the distance. The scene to which the voice belongs, my memory of the burnt earth of wartime devastation, that indescribable conglomeration of greys and that strange smell all seem to be fading just as my eyesight is beginning to dim with the passing years.

My eyes used to be the most perfect part of my body. I was told after my physical examination when I enlisted that I had extraordinarily good eyes. They said if the rest of me were anywhere near as good I'd have been fit for the navy. Now my eyes are no good. Worse, it seems, than just old-age long-sightedness.

In the past my work as a professional union representative required me to spend about ten days a month travelling by train around textile-manufacturing areas. I did this work for many years both before and after the war. In those days the out-of-the way recesses of the third-class carriages were good for reading. I read books, but this did not prevent me from taking in the landscape through the train window. No doubt this was largely due to my good eyesight, though, of course, the atmosphere of these trips was free and relaxed and the trains were pretty slow.

In those days I had to read while I travelled, but I was also very interested in the landscape, customs and people. Most important, I had to be able to understand the people at my journey's end. This is hardly worth mentioning, but when I look back on it now it reminds

57

me of the rather eccentric life I led. For half my poor deprived life my eyes were my only asset; even a weapon perhaps. What I saw with my eyes was mine. Nobody could take that away from me. I could store it away in my heart. I could retrieve it and rearrange it at will. And what's more now I can even listen to that voice calling me from the past.

It happened in the days when my sight was good. I was away on a business trip, early in the summer of 1942. The Pacific War had started on 8th December the previous year. I was in Yamaguchi Prefecture with a colleague. Halfway through our trip we were joined by the chief engineer of the Chūgoku Institute for Fibre Research, located at Fukuyama in Hiroshima Prefecture, and the three of us went to Yanai on the Inland Sea. We spent two days working at the office of the textile union there.

On the third day, at my suggestion, we went across to the little port of Obatake on Suō-Ōshima Island. A white line of surf was breaking a kilometre off-shore on the famous Obatake sandbar. There was a tremendous rumbling noise which seemed to be reverberating up from the ocean floor. The shallows changed with every minute movement of the tide.

We landed at Komatsu harbour and walked several kilometres to the little coastal village of Kuga, to inspect two factories. I say factories, but in fact the owners spent half their time farming and half in manufacture. They had a very rare thread-plying machine. I had discovered this through some old records in the Trade and Industry Department of the Prefectural Office. Perhaps I am becoming a little too technical, but the technique of plying thread, uninteresting as it may appear, is of fundamental importance to the textile industry. At the time there were about thirty various thread-plying machines, both traditional and modern. The top-spinning technique used for the strings of musical instruments, like the *koto* and the *shamisen*, or for surgical thread, and the primitive stretch-twisting technique, both of which are still in use today, I discovered, apparently originated in China. The crepe-weft plying machine known as *mizubatchō* was also originally introduced from China.

Apart from these, western thread-plying machines have been imported since 1873. The one in Suō-Ōshima was an upright *mizubatchō* wheel. The name appeared in the records, but it was something of a phantom in reality.

I wondered why this spinning machine should turn up here on this island in the Inland Sea. Perhaps it had something to do with the processing of the hand-reeled raw silk produced on the island into spun yarn for hand looms. The description "upright" no doubt stemmed from the fact that it operated with the threads running up and down like the strings of a harp, unlike the ordinary *mizubatchō*, in which the twisting was done horizontally. Possibly Suō-Ōshima was the only place where the original form introduced from China still survived.

The first place we visited was on a lonely road some little distance from Komatsu harbour. They were selling cigarettes at the farmhouse and the attached workshop was no longer in use. A young woman, the wife of the owner I suppose, showed us around. A black cow was tethered nearby. An item claimed to be a part of the machine had been pushed into a corner of the room, but it was not possible to visualize the whole from this fragment. However, the wooden pulley attached to the ceiling looked a little different from the traditional Japanese type, so I took a photograph of it.

The second workshop had disappeared altogether. After that, we got directions from one of the locals and, taking a short cut off the main road, we headed for Kuga along a mountain path overlooking the sea. We had crossed two little peaks when an old farmer, wearing a towel over his head, who had been working in a newly-cultivated field, came running over, waving his hands in the air.

"Hey!" he shouted. "Where do you come from?"

Then in the local brogue he told us he had heard that Kyoto had been destroyed in an earthquake and fire and asked if it were true. He said his son was in Kyoto and he had not heard a word from him. He virtually shouted at us to tell him the truth. We assured him we had passed through Kyoto four days before and that nothing like that had happened, but we had great trouble convincing him.

Those were the days when the war situation was developing favourably and we were euphoric over the news of successive victories. As we were climbing the next hill, in an unexpected leap from the imploring words of the old farmer I was suddenly seized by a feeling of disquiet. Perhaps Japan was going to lose. Then, just at that moment, between two small islands visible ahead to our left, I noticed a strange, black shape. We came to a halt.

Apparently there was a naval base in the vicinity and two or three destroyers could be seen this side of the islands. But what was that gigantic shape behind? We stood there side by side staring out over the slightly hazy sea. I was the first to realize. It was an enormous battleship with its bow and stern hidden behind the islands. Its incredible size dwarfed the destroyers in the foreground. "It's the 'Musashi' or the 'Yamato'!"

After a while my colleagues seemed convinced. At the time I found myself recalling the words of the medic at the conscription physical.

— If the battleship we saw was the 64,000 ton "Musashi", then it went down two years later, on 24th October 1944 in the naval battle off the Philippines. It sank, with the loss of many lives, after being hit by over twenty torpedoes and twelve bombs. Or, it may have been the "Yamato", in which case it sank claiming the lives of most of its crew, off Cape Bōnosaki in Kyushu when it was headed south on the special mission for the relief of Okinawa. It was sunk by twelve or more torpedoes and five bombs. —

The spectre of the burnt earth of wartime devastation would assail me from time to time, and not only in my dreams. It would suddenly call me in its deep strong voice, having no regard for what I might be doing; whether I was sitting at my desk or out fishing for *ayu*.[1] The voice did not reproach me, but whenever I sensed it I felt like shutting my eyes and hanging my head. The memory of the battleship we had observed from the hill in Suō-Ōshima affected me in the same way. My younger brother, the one just below me, was killed in Manchuria. He was a private, second-class, in the Army. My next younger brother started out as a crew member on the cruiser "Maya" and spent seven years in the Navy. He remained in the Navy until the end of the War and even now he still retains his naval bearing. That at least is some small consolation. But I cannot escape that strong, deep voice. I won't escape it. On the contrary, I try quietly to recall the scene to engrave it onto my heart. That's to get my own back at the voice. I quietly put it back to sleep again.

It was a scene five months before the defeat. Other things do affect me from time to time, but this scene was different, because I had the feeling I was the first to witness it. I had watched like a spectator. It was sad, ironic I suppose, that my eyes, said to be so much stronger than most, should have so accurately recorded the scene.

But nowadays that my sight is starting to decline it seems the voice is gradually fading away into the distance. It is just a matter of time. I think perhaps I may yet be rescued from it.

---

[1] *Ayu*: Japanese river trout.

# 2

This concerns the bombing of Honjo and Fukagawa on the night of 9 March 1945.

They say it is about a twenty-five-kilometre journey from the village in Tamagawa, where I live, to Nihonbashi in central Tokyo, though I don't know which route they have in mind. It is a further five kilometres from Nihonbashi to Honjo and Fukagawa across the Sumida River. A total of some thirty kilometres altogether. But, it must be closer as the crow flies.

The bomb attack started about twelve o'clock at night, during an air-raid warning for the whole of Tokyo. In the daytime the B29s would take a bearing on Mt Fuji then turn right to attack Tokyo. At night they apparently followed the same flight path, but there were fewer signs of planes passing over my village than in the later May attack on the Yamanote area.

At first, even on the military report over the radio, it was not clear where the attack would come. I remember thinking it strange that they reported soon after, that the target would be the eastern wards of Tokyo. I thought if you are attacking Tokyo it doesn't make much difference where you drop the bombs.

I emerged from the woods and watched the sky over Tokyo. I was wearing my air-raid hood and gaiters. Already, crimson flames were rising in the sky to the east of Tokyo. It was obvious that the B29s were bent on attacking Tokyo east of the Sumida River. The dark forms of the planes caught in the searchlights were heading, one after another, straight into the conflagration scorching the night sky. Relentless shapes pursuing their goal without so much as a sideways glance.

Later, when I saw the records, I discovered that that night there had been three hundred and thirty-four bombers. In that area alone, they had dropped 190,000 incendiary bombs. There had been 125,000 victims, 85,000 of whom had been killed. I could easily see the flames, gradually growing in intensity. My brother-in-law was living in Tsukishima. Several days before, he had loaded what luggage he needed for evacuation into a large hand-cart and pulled it all the way to our village. With him was his eldest son, a lad in junior high school. My elder sister had already taken the baby and evacuated to our parents' home in Shinshū. The two of them ate some steamed potatoes with us then headed straight back home, pulling the empty cart. They were in a hurry to get back before nightfall. I thought perhaps Tsukishima had also been caught in the bombing. When I first came to Tokyo, like some poor stray dog, my brother-in-law had helped me, without even telling my sister. It's one thing to have one's house burnt down, but.... The bombing was long and persistent. Against the backdrop of the crimson sky the gigantic silver bodies of the B29s shone eerily as if bathed in blood. Some flew surprisingly low as they crawled through the sky. I watched feeling utterly powerless to do anything.

The little flashes of the interceptor fighter planes threading their way through the searchlight beams mingled with the flights of bombers. I don't know when the bombing actually finished. Even after the air-raid alarm had been revoked, the flames continued to burn the night sky. I took off my gaiters and slept for a while. The office where I worked was in Nihonbashi, near Sakinomori shrine in Horidome. A close friend of mine was there on night duty. I was worried about him too. I also knew three or four people with houses in the downtown area. In the morning I strapped on my gaiters and left the house carrying my air-raid hood and a steel helmet over my shoulder. I took a lunch box with enough potato and rice mix for two meals. I made sure I had plenty of salted plums. It must have been about 6.30. The local train was running. I got out at Shinjuku and took the national rail to Kanda station. It was peculiar how the scene inside the train and outside the window was no different from usual. How could that be! It was not until I got out at Kanda station that the actual experience of the bombing came home to me. Groups of victims flooded the station and the surrounding area.

Everyone was black with smoke and ash. Some were wearing charred air-raid hoods. Right next to the ticket wicket was a half-naked man wearing a black iron pot on his head. His skin from the waist up was red, from burns no doubt. First he did not strike me as being particularly different from any of the other victims in the crowd. Then I suddenly realized his mind had been deranged by the shock. There was a woman like that too. She was normally dressed, wearing baggy peasant trousers, but she was standing there blankly propped against a pillar in the station, solicitously nursing a long household broom with a singed brush. Perhaps she had been using it for support.

I hurried in the direction of Suginomori shrine. Buildings here and there had been burnt, but my office had escaped. From there I walked by the shortest route to Akaishi-chō, in Tsukiji. I had in mind to take the Tsukuda ferry as a short cut across to Tsukishima. If that proved impossible I had intended to cross the Sumida River at Eitaibashi or Kachidokibashi. The boatman was alive. Only two or three people were on the Tsukuda ferry. Nobody uttered a word. When we reached the opposite bank I raced off the boat. In Tsukuda the road I always walked along was unchanged. Tsukishima too, I discovered on my arrival, had been spared. I was overjoyed it was safe, of course, but it felt very curious.

My brother-in-law and his boy both had red, inflamed eyes. He could not understand how no bombs had fallen this side of Aioibashi, the long bridge linking Fukagawa-Etchōjima with Tsukudajima. The merchant marine college was on the Fukagawa side of the bridge.

I left my brother-in-law's place and once again found myself alone. For a while I just stood there in the middle of the road. It was not yet

10 o'clock. I was in two minds whether to go back over Kachidokibashi towards Tsukiji and then take the train or subway home, or to go and see someone I knew in Honjo-Ryōgoku. But on second thoughts I recalled that my friend in Ryōgoku had evacuated with his family a week or so earlier to a spot near Ōme in Okutama. I started walking, having decided to return via Kachidokibashi.

That morning not a soul was to be seen on the street. The area usually had a real downtown feel about it, especially at night with its rows of street stalls. Perhaps the locals were asleep, having collapsed exhausted from the night of tension and struggle which had lasted until just before dawn. Or perhaps the houses were deserted. Suddenly I changed my mind, turned on my heel and started walking towards Aioibashi. No doubt the dead, blackened street had made me change my mind.

I came out on the main road with the tram tracks. There was no sign of anybody there either. Of course, the trams were not running. From Tsukishima I crossed Hatsumibashi bridge to Tsukudajima. The next long bridge was Aioibashi. There was a cold sea breeze blowing. I was coming close to Monzen-nakachō in Fukagawa. The road crossed Fukagawa, Honjo and then from around Komagatabashi and Asaibashi turned right towards Narihira and Oshiage.

Even beyond Aioibashi a few houses were left standing. I was feeling slightly more relaxed, having discovered that my brother-in-law's house had escaped the bombing. From about this point the spent shells of incendiary bombs became conspicuous in the broad thoroughfare. They looked like the long cylinders used for housing sutra scrolls. They were scattered everywhere. And then I saw the first corpse. It was a naked woman. She had fallen diagonally across the edge of the footpath. There was a faint wisp of smoke covering her face, but she was a cold, pale colour as if her whole body had been skinned. I presumed this was due to the strength of the blast. She just had one white *tabi* sock on her left foot. I stopped, feeling I should cover her with one of the burnt sheets of corrugated iron which had floated down onto the road. But, I soon realized charred corpses were lying here and there all about me. There was even a woman wearing a striped silk air-raid hood like mine. I was the only living, moving being there.

I broke into a trot and reached Monzen-nakachō. The destruction was gradually becoming worse. It was only then that I came across three or four people. They must have been locals, I suppose. There was no sign anywhere of the fire brigade or rescue services. I should have turned left and gone home, but I did not. Like a sleepwalker I continued on straight ahead down the main road. I crossed a small bridge. From there I was able to gaze out over the vast expanse of burnt earth of Fukagawa and Honjo. Smoke was still rising here and there. Even the road had been burnt and I imagined I could feel the latent heat. The number of corpses progressively increased. In the ash-grey piles of burnt earth only the human remains, swollen and different in colour, stood out from the rest of the burnt debris. I do not remember whether the sky was clear or cloudy. A slight breeze was blowing, stirring up the ash along the road. Here and there a few people were moving about like sleepwalkers. It seemed strange that they had survived.

Several times I thought of going back home. Many bodies were floating with the burnt debris in the canal. One of them, hands clinging to the stone, seemed to be trying to scramble out. The eyes were open and I thought perhaps it was alive. Just past Midorichō, I came upon a spectacle which left me petrified. The place had apparently been a bicycle shop. There were several burnt bicycles lying around. In front of the bicycles three charred bodies were standing. The tallest was obviously the father. One of the two children was clinging to his chest, the other to his knees. They looked like an ash-grey sculpture. I felt that one touch would have instantly turned them to dust.

I had lost the ability to shed tears. I continued on a little further and finally turned left at the Ishihara-chō intersection, just beside the Earthquake Memorial Hall. I crossed the Sumida River at Kuramaebashi bridge. Upstream through the smoke I could see the bridges of Umayabashi and Azumabashi. I squatted down on the charred bridge and brought up a little yellow bile. I took a deep breath. Even the breeze over the river smelled burnt. It was just before noon.

*

# Road Through the Snow

By Minakami Tsutomo
Translated by Hugh Clarke

## 1

The woman wore a striped apron over her sweater which was
beginning to fray at the collar. She had reached the age where she
stooped with the effort of getting the horses out of the snow-locked
stables.

Letting the tether fall slack to the ground she led Suiroku to the
corner of the yard and, after patting his belly two or three times,
tethered him to a stake. She heaved a sigh and looked up to the sky.

Where a naked larch forest bore down behind the stables, the short
rays of sunshine filtered through the treetops like rain. The sun would
set by three o'clock. Usually she put the horses out before noon. The
horse was frisky, quivering with excitement. From time to time it
tossed its head and snorted. It trotted around in a large circle at the end
of the ample tether the woman had provided, occasionally kicking up
the snow with its forelegs and bucking. Once or twice, it dropped a
pat the size of a large dinner plate.

The father's funeral had been on 7th January. Last winter he had put
the horses out by himself. He would tether the five horses outside,
replace the straw in the sleeping stalls and wash out the feed buckets.
The last time I saw him, he was washing the feet of an old bay.
Down on one knee with the horse's hoof in his lap and his head under
its belly, he was virtually nursing the hoof as he tapped away at the
underside with a bamboo spatula. I had heard he had gone into the
Ueda hospital at the end of autumn, though he died on 3rd January.

They had held the funeral on the seventh. The townsfolk said it was lung cancer. It was around the time of the funeral that his wife had taken over the task of putting out the horses. That was when the daughter began to appear on the scene. I heard that her mother had called her back home from a college in Tokyo. Around the beginning of February the daughter, who was small, but with well-chiselled features, gallantly began to busy herself helping with chores around the house. She too wore an old sweater under her apron-like work clothes, tied at the waist with a thin cord. She led out the next horse after her mother and, just as her mother had done, wound the tether rope around another stake some distance from the first. She did it very expertly, no doubt having observed the operation since childhood, then went straight back into the stable. The second horse was also in high spirits. I was expecting it to run around in a big circle too, but it suddenly crouched down, rubbed its belly against the ground, then rolled over. It thrust out all four legs in what appeared to be a stretch, then repeatedly rubbed its head into the snow. It seems horses like fresh snow. It was very unusual for the mother to put out five horses as the father had done. It was usually just one or two, three at the most. The days were short and there was no man to help. Cleaning out three stables a day was all the mother and daughter could manage. I often saw them run off to the compost shed carrying the largest possible armfuls of steaming sleeping straw from the stables. Even their faces got dirty doing this job. They would work away until their pulled-back hair became quite dishevelled. Their house appeared lower than any other, partly because the earth had been dug out a step below ground level to build the stables. When snow collected on the roof it would mingle with the snow banked up on the side of the road by the dump trucks, making it look as if the house were buried in snow. I enjoyed watching the scene without a soul in sight anywhere, save just here on the plateau by the larch forest where mother, daughter and the horses were moving about outside. There was just one black Kiso horse. The others were three greys and a white horse, which the locals said was an Arab-Norman cross. The Kiso black, with a short-cropped mane and small ears, must have been four or five years old. But it too resembled the crossbreeds with its bulging belly and ridiculously short legs. My home town is Wakasa. When I was a boy horse-drawn ploughs were still popular, so I had often seen short horses like that. They were cart horses bred in Hokkaido and Aomori. Compared to the elegant race horse with its slim, taut body and long legs, these horses were quite unprepossessing. Nevertheless, I preferred them because they were placid and reliable, despite their clumsy appearance. Thoroughbreds invariably appear aloof and arrogant.

## 2

Whenever the snow stopped and the sun came out, I would leave the house and walk over towards that single dwelling. Some days there were no horses outside, but even so I would stop for a while when I was passing the house. Through breaks in the surrounding snow bank you could see into the stables. The five horses would be facing me looking towards the entrance of their bays across a metre-wide strip of concrete. They would rub their necks against the cross-pole and pound the ground with their feet, looking very much as if they wanted to go outside. On such occasions there was never any sign of mother or daughter at the house. Apparently they had gone out somewhere in the van the daughter drove.

When the father was alive they had set aside an area next to the entrance hall as an office. It was often filled with customers, but now the room was rarely opened and the curtains remained drawn. When it was snowing, they kept the light on there even in the daytime.

In summer the highland town was bustling with people escaping the heat. The holiday cottages were occupied too. The commercial district of the township was on the far side of the forest near the by-pass on the road which ran past the house where the mother and daughter lived. In July and August the area was filled with young cycling enthusiasts. The locals said there must be a good three hundred shops just counting those which were branches of Tokyo stores, but all of these closed their doors at the end of autumn and spent the winter in desolation with their entrances boarded up. This scene clearly revealed the fickle emotions of city folk. The area around the mother and daughter's riding club was always quiet, given the fact that the locals lived scattered over a wide area and the club was beyond the forest some distance from the shops.

Having looked to see which particular type of horse was tethered outside that day and watched mother and daughter going about the stables and yards, I walked off through the larch forest behind the house in the direction of the M. Hotel. The hotel, situated high up on a plateau, in the middle of a forest of pines, was an unusual timber building in the western style, which had started business in the early years of the Meiji period. It often appeared in etchings in magazines, but in winter it too used to be closed most of the time. Since I started spending my winters here three years ago, they have begun to keep some of the guest rooms open on weekends and generally the grill stays open all the time. There are two Catholic churches in the area and I've heard that there has been an increase in the numbers of young people being married there, so the hotel takes reservations from newlyweds who book the church and hotel together. Sometimes, when it was snowing or something, I would see young couples, but the hotel was hardly ever full. The peace and quiet of this hotel appealed to me, so I would always make it the destination of my walks. In this way I had got to know by sight the bellboys and the girls working in the dining-room. The manager, a man called Tokonami, was a genial fellow of about sixty with a head of white hair. Sometimes he would be sitting alone at a table in the grill. Whenever I went there he would draw up a chair beside me and have a cup of coffee himself.

When I opened the conversation with, "The mother and daughter at the Matsutani riding school work hard, don't they?" He replied, "Yes, I admire the way the girl just threw in her college studies." He praised the daughter, then he explained that there seemed to be some other reason why, after her father died, she had suddenly given up college just short of her graduation. He went on to say that you don't find daughters these days who are prepared to stay and look after the horses. "Do you know? It was old man Matsutani who started off riding clubs in this town. He was a great authority on horses. During the occupation he had twenty of them. He really used to love horses." Tokonami talked as if he had been very close to Matsutani Yonezō before he died. Then he said, "Horses are funny, you know. Apparently they fatten them up through the winter, then cut back their feed in the summer when they are hired out for riding."

I thought the reverse would be true. It would be only common-sense to fill them up on days when they were expending energy carrying customers around. But it seems Matsutani Yonezō, through long years of experience, noticed that mixed breeds tended to become flighty when allowed to eat their fill, so he restricted their feed. This reduced their energy and made them more placid mounts for women and children. That's the reason it was generally accepted that Matsutani's horses were more gentle than those of other stables. I was listening to all this with great interest as I had not heard it before. "But with the old man's training programme it's a terrible job caring for the horses in winter. You know, the woman feeds them five times a day. She gets up at five. Apparently if she sleeps in the horses demand their feed by kicking the boards of the stables. Then she feeds them again at noon, then at three o'clock, nine o'clock and again at eleven o'clock. That's a total of five times a day! Of course, the three o'clock and nine o'clock feeds are really just snacks: a little hay and some water. All the other feeds have to be hay and oats mixed together and water with added calcium, otherwise, the old man used to say, the horses would shake their heads in protest. That's extravagance for you! In winter neither mother nor daughter can get a decent night's sleep." I was disturbed to learn just how busy the mother and daughter were. "I suppose this year they'll employ a student part-time, but the daughter will probably still have to walk along holding the bridle. The village office is concerned over the mountain of letters they have been getting about horses fouling the roads, so things are going to become pretty tight from now on as far as horse-riding is concerned." After saying all this Tokonami asked, "Do you like horses?" I felt I could not really say I liked them and, of course, I had never actually ridden one. But anyway I answered, "Yes, I do."

Having been asked so unexpectedly I was not able to explain it clearly, but two or three incidents came to mind.

## 3

About thirteen years ago in the summer I first rented a house here in the highlands, my second daughter, who is crippled in the legs, was with us. She was three years old at the time. She has congenital spina bifida and was born with a deformation of the spine. She had an operation soon after birth and they were able to straighten the spine, but during the procedure the surgeon made a mistake and severed a nerve, which resulted in loss of feeling in several places from the waist down. Below the knees, particularly from the ankle to the tips of the toes, her legs were virtually dead. The feet just hung limp and did not grow with the rest of her body. My wife, concerned the girl would have to spend the rest of her life in a wheelchair, discussed the matter with a doctor, who eventually performed an operation which would enable our daughter to get around on crutches. The procedure involved transplanting bone matter from my wife into the child's undeveloped pelvic region. It was the summer after the operation, so I remember it well.

Horses often went past the house. They used to fascinate our daughter. We'd take her out to the gate in her wheelchair to watch them. Once ten or so filed past, all being ridden by young men, women and children. Students on vacation work were leading them along by the bridle. They were all horses from the Matsutani riding club. In those days, there was none of the competition there is now and the Matsutanis must have had a monopoly on the business. The stables were not out on the new highway then, but in an area right in the middle of town near the station. That was because the house they rented was nearby and the tourist riding course approved by the town office, ran down that particular road. My daughter had been badgering me to let her have a ride on a horse. She reasoned that with a bad leg she should at least be able to ride a horse. My wife was against it. Understandably so. It would have been irresponsible to have the child sit in the saddle without the full use of her legs. Even if they did let her ride, her mother would have to go along with her all the way and she would no doubt get in the way of the horse boy. My wife managed to mollify her. In the end, it was decided that instead of the horse-ride, they would go to have a look at the horses at the stables. They set off with my wife pushing the wheelchair. My daughter came back satisfied having seen a stable full of unusually coloured horses. As we were talking about this my wife said, "She liked the white mare, Hanako." Apparently there was only one white horse, an old mare in a stall bearing a plaque with the name, "Hanako". "We weren't sure if she'd let us pat her, so I asked the old man and he said it would be all right. Then, you know, horses are uncanny. Hanako

74

came up and rubbed its nose against her. She did not even cry, but just sat there stroking its wet dribbling nose. I know you don't like horses, but don't you think that's wonderful!"

I had no particular dislike for horses, despite my wife's comment. After that my daughter went to see the horses every day. When my wife did not go, my wife's elder sister, who was helping with the nursing, would take her. One day my daughter came home and reported, "Hanako does not kick, anyway!" This retort was for the benefit of her mother who had yelled to her sister as she set off pushing the wheelchair. "She kicks if you get too close. Be careful!" That summer I was busy with my work and did not once take my daughter to the riding club. There was no other reason. I had been thinking I would take her one day, but before I knew it autumn had come. Apparently this also led to my wife's concluding that I disliked horses.

## 4

In May 1944 I had received my conscription orders and was working as a groom with the 43rd Army Corps in Fushimi. In those days they used to call the grooms special service soldiers, but the formal military term was "auxiliary transport soldier". I spent three terrible months looking after these animals, wondering all the while why, faced with the prospect of imminent defeat, the army continued to train so many young horses. From morning till night we would be washing down the horses, drying out dung-covered straw and cleaning out the stables. Each soldier had to look after three horses. My horses were not too bad, but some of my comrades had pretty wild ones and injuries were frequent. It was when we were giving the horses their late afternoon drink, that private second-class Kobayashi Chōkichi was killed in an accident. I remember the day well.

75

In front of each of the five stables we had in our unit there was an area for watering the horses; long, narrow troughs were filled with tap water. I do not know why the watering area was so crowded that evening. I suppose it was congested because we soldiers disregarded any idea of taking turns and vied with each other in getting our charges out of the stables and first to the drinking troughs. Another factor was the spiteful soldier we had on duty that evening. Everyone was agitated and horses and men alike were frantically bustling around on both sides of the troughs.

Private Kobayashi moved in after his friend private Ōtani had finished. Pulling down the head of his horse Shikishima, he took a firm grip on the bridle and signalled to the man and horse on his left that he was about to squeeze through to the trough. At the same time private Watanabe pushed in leading Ōyashima.

Then, suddenly Ōyashima turned full circle forcing Kobayashi into Ayanishiki on his right. It was just getting dark. Kobayashi stumbled and fell against the trough. As he was regaining his feet he found himself looking straight at the rump of Ōyashima which had just defecated. In his surprise Kobayashi let go of Shikishima's reins and fell. At that instant Shikishima threw back his head and broke out of line. It was only at that one moment that Kobayashi screamed. When I looked he was sprawled out on the ground five metres away. He was lying on his back shouting something, when suddenly he stretched out his arms as if making a "banzai" cheer and fell motionless still looking upwards. I could not go to him as I was putting my horse back into its stall. Shikishima, the horse which had kicked Kobayashi had run off stirring up the dust to the east of the stables. The duty watch called out, "Horse loose. Watch out!" Some of us then ran over to Kobayashi. He said nothing. Blood was gushing from a large split in his forehead, which looked for all the world as if it had been staved in with a hatchet.

We bade farewell to private Kobayashi there under the purple sky as he was being carried off to the medical room on a stretcher. That stretcher disappearing into the company headquarters was the last we were to see of him.

After that we were more careful at watering time, but you can imagine the thoughts which passed through my mind every day for three months when I ran my horses up to the water trough. It was only after I left the army that I heard Kobayashi had died. We common soldiers were never told that he had died on the fourth day after the accident.

## 5

I had never mentioned this incident from my old horse-handling days to my wife or child. I know there are many fathers who boast about their exploits during the war, but I have absolutely nothing I can boast about. In fact, when I think of my colleagues, they were all short, either one-eyed, or hunch-backed or with fingers missing. There were even three rehabilitated consumptives like me. We had all been recruited from C and D grade second-class conscripts who had been working in the provinces. Our platoon leader frequently reminded us that we were the absolute riff-raff as soldiers. Even the real soldiers, living as they were removed from military action, were not likely to have any decent stories to tell. Besides, people at large found the idea of being a horse-handler somewhat curious and would listen to my stories with a smile. I felt no inclination to talk if I was just going to be laughed at. From time to time I recalled the second-class private who was kicked to death by a horse at watering time. Not when I was talking to people, but when I was alone doing nothing in particular, the memory would come back. Once, however, I had thought that with the passing of time, the events of my horse-handling days were virtually being erased from my memory. It was strange, but apparently this belief stemmed from a general human desire to forget bad times. I suppose it is only natural to dislike depressing memories.

So, I was upset at my wife's words, "She's not like you!" after she had explained how thrilled our daughter had been at being able to pat Hanako's nose. I had not yet met my wife when I was a horse-handler in the army. In those days I was still married to the mother of my eldest daughter. I was separated from her some years after the defeat and married my present wife. Come to think of it, my first wife knew all about my work as a horse-handler. Now and then (it was just before we broke up) she would speak to others with obvious disdain about the section of the army into which I had been conscripted. That's why I did not say much about my army experiences to my second wife. I suppose, too, that the reason I found it difficult to reply when Tokonami from the hotel asked me if I liked horses was that the memory of these animals still lurks in my subconscious. The sight of the dark blood gushing from the split in the forehead of my comrade-in-arms (a slight exaggeration perhaps, considering he had died as a horse groom on home duty) would always remain there buried under the ground snow of my memory.

# 6

I spent this winter walking. Whenever I had a spare moment, I would go to see the stables where the mother and daughter were. But I had never once spoken to them. Sometimes a white horse or a chestnut would be striding out joyfully over the paddock, a sheet of silver in the sunlight. Or mother and daughter would be laughing and enjoying themselves throwing snow over the horses. At times like that I really felt like saying something to them. I wondered, for example, if the solitary white horse they had was the same Hanako my daughter had taken a shine to thirteen years before. Sometimes I felt that the horse could not have been more than twenty, which would have made it a bit young to be the Hanako of thirteen years ago. Yet on other days I felt she looked very old and might very well be Hanako. I was also aware that they did not put the white horse out in the paddock very often and I wanted to ask about that too. Yet there was a certain aura surrounding this mother and daughter which did not appear to welcome strangers. It would not be long until the busy summer season when, with the father dead, the mother would have to take on the responsibility of running the place. That is why they had to feed the horses well and fatten them up during the winter. Mother and daughter were making preparations for the coming of summer. No doubt the mother was also thinking up plans for the future of her daughter who had sacrificed her college studies to come back home. I had no qualms about probing the inner workings of the family in my imagination, but I had no inclination to actually question them about it.

It was the third year I had spent the winter here with just me and the housekeeper. My wife and children were in Tokyo. My second daughter was in her third year of junior high school and now very rarely came to this mountain resort. She was attending the Metropolitan Special School for the Disabled in Setagaya. She could now use crutches, thanks to the fervent prayers of her mother, but we still usually relied on the wheelchair. So my wife had to be with her all the time. Just the other day, I returned home to attend to some business, only to find that my wife and daughter were away at the hospital. I came straight back to the mountains and that evening I had a phone call from my wife. "What brought you home?", she asked. I said there was nothing in particular, but that since I was back in Tokyo I felt I would like to say hello to my daughter. When I asked what they had said at the hospital my wife replied, "The doctor says she has every illness you can think of. I'm telling you, the child and I are absolutely worn out!" Apparently it had been just the regular periodical examination at the hospital, but recently our daughter had developed kidney trouble. Since the nerves in the bladder region are dead, she has been going to school with an artificial bladder. It seems that with the fully-developed upper-part of the body unable to be supported by the withered legs, problems occur with the internal organs as their functions reach maturity. She is in the unfortunate position where the more rigorous the growth in her body the greater the affected area becomes. My wife's words no doubt stemmed from the fact that she was putting herself in the place of the child whose suffering was being compounded twice or three times over. On the few occasions when I am back home, I feel I want to see my daughter too. But the sight of the girl with the upper body of an adult crawling around because her legs can no longer support her weight... I leave all that to my wife and come up here to the mountains.

The people in the village had been saying there was a lot of snow this year. Sometimes it fell for two or three days on end. At night the wind would howl and rattle the shutters. Usually on nights like that I would just sit at my desk in the study doing nothing, vacantly mulling over my thoughts. I am fourteen years older than my present wife. In twelve years time when I am seventy, my wife will be fifty-six and still, no doubt, be caring for a disabled daughter of twenty-seven. I did not feel confident that I would live beyond seventy, or perhaps I was not really being honest with myself there. When I was in the army I was prepared to be sent abroad to die with my horses. Actually, seven days before I left, a unit of my colleagues set out from Shimonoseki on a transport vessel which came under fire off the coast of Taiwan and was sunk, killing the lot of them. They did not have time to escape because they were down in the hold with the horses. Somehow I was demobbed while waiting to be sent on the next transport ship. So I survived. I felt as if it was a bonus that I was still alive now at the age of fifty-eight. If I were to reach seventy surely that would be enough. That is how I really felt, but whether I reached seventy or not, I sometimes wondered how my wife and disabled child would manage after my death. I had not even gone to the operation thirteen years before when they had transplanted bone from my wife to enable my daughter to walk on crutches. I had blamed my work. What a selfish father I had been. I say that even while I am away I am thinking of them and so on, but in the final analysis something in my character tells me I should be enjoying myself in the bonus years I have left to live. I dislike confronting the unpalatable. I close my eyes and flee as quickly as possible. Who on earth, I wonder, would I have been prepared to slice off some of my own bone for.

## 7

From about the middle of February the temperature rose suddenly and there were even some days when it seemed the ground snow would thaw, but then after the twentieth we had another cold spell. Of course, they say that usually the coldest time is towards the end of February. Again the mountains were covered in snow right down to the foothills and even in the sparse forest, where the dirt had been showing through here and there between the trees, the ground was a blanket of silver. One afternoon on a day like this the grey clouds parted slightly and the pale sun seemed to be shining through, so as usual I donned my thick coat and gum boots and went out. Naturally, I set out for the Matsutani place, but just before I was about to turn into the main road, going down between the larch forest and the reclaimed land with its carefully pruned young pines I noticed in the snow covering the two ruts of the road the clear imprints of a horse's hooves. I came to a halt. There could be no doubt that not so long before a horse had gone along this road travelling in the same direction I was walking. You did not have to be an expert to recognize the hoof prints. Here and there the prints seemed to indicate that the horse had thrust its forelegs firmly into the snow then swept them back spraying out a shower of snow as it went. There could be no doubt they were the prints of joy and elation of the horse which had been chosen to leave the narrow confines of the stable. But wait! The thought suddenly struck me. The horse could not be walking alone. Someone had led it. The mother perhaps. No, more likely the daughter. I once again trained my eyes on the road with its distinct hoof prints, to see if I could find a human footprint as well. Sure enough, I found one. I would say it was about a size seven and a half. The boot print, evident from the wavy pattern on its rubber sole, ran along the ridge like an acrobat walking a tight rope, jutting out slightly in places, elsewhere showing a full clear outline on the crest. Ah, it is the daughter, I thought. These prints are not likely to continue far. But anyway, it seems very strange that the girl whom I've hardly ever seen walking the horses should decide to go out walking a horse today. Perhaps the horses are bored with being cooped up in the stables throughout the long snow-bound winter months and she has decided to start walking them one at a time. Yes, that must be it. With these thoughts in mind I quickened my pace and followed the tracks. After a while the gum boot and hoof tracks came to a cross-road and turned right. To the right the road ran through a pine grove on a gentle slope then down into a valley. From here it was virgin snow. There were just four dotted lines, the prints of the girl and the horse. Naturally, I hurried off in the same direction. The pine forest gave way to a wood of larch trees. The road runs downhill, but if you continue on, you finally come to the red pine forest of the Minamigaoka hills, where, according to local gossip, the Crown Prince is said to have a villa. I thought that if you continued down that way, you must end up in quite the opposite direction to the by-pass, near the old air force barracks, which is now a vast area of pasture land. How far down had the girl and the horse gone? I wanted to find them quickly. I walked faster, hurrying on through an area devoid of houses. In the forest of assorted trees which covered the hills chestnut and oak trees had their branches broken or the bark removed in places exposing the bare trunks underneath. A giant pine with half its trunk scorched by lightning, barely alive, thrust through the even surface formed by the bare treetops below and from around its massive roots numerous black-winged birds flew off in succession.

It was a quiet road and there was no sign of people. How far had the girl gone on leading the horse? My heart was pounding in my desire to catch up with her quickly. Then I saw her. It was just as I came out of the bare forest of larch trees and I turned my gaze from the thick blanket of firs on the hill to the open moorland which had suddenly come into view. But it was not just the girl as I had imagined. She was riding on the horse's back. It was the mother who was leading the horse. Daughter riding and mother leading, through a field of silvery white like a pastel painting in red and black on white art paper. The daughter was wearing baggy farmer's trousers under her red sweater. Bent forward just slightly with her tightly pulled-back hair trailing out behind her, her profile showed composure as she held the reins. From time to time the mother would look up at her daughter, then immediately look down again as she led the horse by the bridle. Suiroku's reins were stretched taut between the mother and the horse. No sooner would the sun come out than it would cloud over again. Captured by the snow clouds the sun would shrink into a little coppery ball and lose its light, but the vast field remained forever white.

The horse appeared to be the chestnut roan. From time to time the girl used the reins to quicken its pace. Determined not to fall behind the horse the mother walked with her back bent and her face thrust forward. Westward further westward mother and daughter crossed the moor.

# Note on the Authors

**Arishima Takeo** (1878-1923) achieved fame during his own lifetime as an author and social critic. He was born into a Satsuma samurai family and was educated initially at the Sapporo Agricultural College where he became a Christian and later at Haverford College in Philadelphia. After his wife and father died in 1916 he abandoned teaching as a career and became a full-time writer. By this time he had also given up his faith. "The Death of Osue" was first published in 1914, at the end of that period when he was just beginning to make a name as an author. It is set in Sapporo where he had been teaching English since 1908. Among his most celebrated works are *The Descendant of Cain* (1917) and the work recognized as his masterpiece *A Certain Woman* (1918).

**Minakami Tsutomu**, the son of an impoverished coffin-maker, was born in Fukui prefecture in 1919. Minakami worked variously as a shop assistant, pedlar and debt collector before enrolling into the Japanese literature department at Ritsumeikan University. In 1938, he abandoned his university studies without graduating and went to Manchuria. While abroad Minakami became ill and was compelled to return home where he spent a year and a half in convalescence. Although he penned his maiden work, *Song of the Frying Pan*, just after the war, the need to earn a living kept Minakami from literary activity until 1959 when he re-emerged with *Mist and Shadows*, a novel on the Japanese Communist Party. Minakami's reputation as a major writer became firmly established when he won the Naoki Prize for his semi-autobiographical novel on temple life, *Temple of the Wild Geese*, in 1961. He has published numerous detective stories and historical novels and counts the Kikuchi Kan Prize and the Tanizaki Prize among his literary awards. "Road Through the Snow", published in 1976, a very personal, introspective story, falls into the traditional genre of the I-novel.

**Nakajima Atsushi** (1909-1942). His works comprising some seventeen short stories and a handful of novels, are perhaps not sufficient in quantity to rank the author among the major writers of modern Japan, but there are some works, particularly among the short stories, which are very highly rated indeed by both literary critics and the general readers of today. "Happiness" was published in 1942 in a collection of stories entitled *Tales of the South Seas*, written soon after his return from duties as an official of the Ministry of Education in Palau. "The Mummy" was included in another collection produced in the same year. Soon after its publication, Nakajima died of asthma at the age of thirty-three in December 1942.

**Shimamura Toshimasa** was born in Nagano in 1912. His maiden work, a long novel, *Koreans*, about a community of Korean gravel miners, was serialized in *Bungakusha* from July 1940 to May 1941. The work was widely acclaimed and Shimamura was nominated as a candidate for the Akutagawa Prize. Employed full-time in the textile industry, Shimamura nevertheless managed to maintain a regular output of short stories all of which display simplicity in content and style combined with a polished artistry and purity of language. In "Sumida River", published in March 1976, Shimamura explores the themes of age, memory and the war using the traditional Japanese techniques of the travel diary as he describes in minute detail his progress along the Sumida River after the bombing raid of 9 March 1945.

**Tsuji Kunio** was born in Tokyo in 1925. He graduated from Tokyo University with a major in French literature and later taught

French at three other universities in Tokyo. Basing himself in Paris, he lived in Europe from 1957 to 1961. It was during his European sojourn that he established himself as a novelist. "The Distant Garden" was written in 1945 when he was only twenty and was his maiden work of fiction. Since then he has written numerous short stories, novels (including multi-volume historical novels), travelogues and essays. He has received a number of major literary awards.

**Yoshiyuki Junnosuke** was born in Okayama in 1924 the eldest son of the writer Yoshiyuki Eisuke. The family moved to Tokyo when Junnosuke was three. At the outbreak of the Pacific War he moved to Shizuoka where he attended high school. A respiratory illness contracted around this time left him unfit for military service. After the war he entered the English literature department of Tokyo University, but soon became so involved in literary activity, contributing to various coterie magazines like *Ashi*, *Sedai* and *Shinshichō*, that he eventually discontinued his studies in 1947 without graduating. He made his literary debut in 1950 with *The Rose-Seller* and was awarded the prestigious Akutagawa prize for *Showers* in 1954. "Three Policemen" was published in 1974.

# Note on the Translators

Professor H. D. B. Clarke holds the Chair of Japanese Studies and is Head of the Department of East Asian Studies at the University of Sydney. Dr Sakuko Matsui is Associate Professor and Dr Leith Morton is Senior Lecturer in Japanese in the same Department.

Professor Clarke is co-author of *Colloquial Japanese* (RKP, 1981) and has written a number of articles on Okinawan society, language and literature.

Dr Sakuko Matsui is the author of *Natsume Sōseki As a Critic of English Literature* (Centre for East Asian Studies, 1975) and co-translator of Tanizaki Jun'ichirō's *A Cat, Shōzō and Two Women* (Wild Peony, 1988).

Dr Leith Morton is the author of *Divided Self: A Biography of Arishima Takeo* (Allen & Unwin, 1988), translator of Kusano Shinpei's *Mt Fuji: Selected Poems, 1943-1986* (Katydid/Oakland University Press, 1991) and has written various articles on modern Japanese fiction and poetry.

88

Also published by Wild Peony:

• *Shijin: Autobiography of the Poet Kaneko Mitsuharu, 1895-1975*
Translations and introduction by A. R. Davis
Edited by A. D. Syrokomla-Stefanowska
University of Sydney East Asian Series No. 1
324 pp. ISBN 0 9590735 3 1

• Tanizaki Jun'ichiro, *A Cat, Shozo and Two Women*
Translated by Matsui Sakuko
University of Sydney East Asian Series No. 2
150 pp. ISBN 0 9590735 5 8

• Yang Lian, *Masks and Crocodile: A Contemporary Chinese Poet and His Poetry*
Translations and introduction by Mabel Lee
Illustrations by Li Liang
University of Sydney East Asian Series No. 3
146 pp. ISBN 0 9590735 7 4

• Kam Louie, *Between Fact and Fiction: Essays on Post-Mao Chinese Literature and Society*
144 pp. ISBN 0 9590735 6 6

• *Readings in Modern Chinese*
Compiled by Liu Wei-ping, Mabel Lee, A. J. Prince, Lily Shaw Lee and R. S. W. Hsu
161 pp. ISBN 0 9590735 4 X

• *Basic Chinese Grammar and Sentence Patterns*
A. D. Syrokomla-Stefanowska and Mabel Lee
99 pp. ISBN 0 9590735 1 5

• *Putonghua: A Practical Course in Spoken Chinese*
Mabel Lee and Zhang Wu-ai
101 pp. ISBN 0 9590735 0 7

International Distribution:
University of Hawaii Press, 2840 Kolowalu Street, Honolulu, Hawaii 96822
FAX: (808)988-6052

Available in Australia from:
Wild Peony Book Publishers, PO Box 636 Broadway NSW 2007; FAX: (02)763 1320